HILARY MANTEL [...]cluding *A Place of Greater S[...] d Black*, which was shortlisted for the 2006 Orange Prize and, most recently, *Wolf Hall*, winner of the 2009 Man Booker Prize.

From the reviews of *Fludd*:

'A faultless comic masterpiece' AUBERON WAUGH

'*Fludd* is a funny, exquisitely written story of priests and nuns in fifties England, but it is also a questioning, intellectual book that applies a profound thoughtfulness to various abstruse areas of religious (or supernatural) belief ... This is a novel about transformation – the sort of transformation that counts, in the Gospels, as miracle. But the figure who works the transformations is not the Messiah; he is Fludd, a reincarnated seventeenth-century alchemist who turns up mysteriously one dark and stormy night in the tough, gritty, superstitious northern town of Fetherhoughton' *Literary Review*

'In *Fludd* Hilary Mantel draws on her imagination, inventing a dark universe which works to laws of her own making. The effect is dazzling, and establishes her in the front rank of novelists writing in England today' JOAN SMITH, *Guardian*

'The setting is as melancholy as ever: it is the familiar dismal, sinister world, where the oppressors are shadowy and monolithic, the victims pathetic, evil and crazed, but it is no longer the real world. Instead, it is the realm of fable, and in fables, however dark things appear, there are always fairy godmothers or even angels to come to the rescue ... Small miracles begin to happen; none of them particularly holy ... Good morality tales are unusual; but rarer still are books that genuinely make you laugh aloud' *Spectator*

'In *Fludd*, Hilary Mantel brings together the miraculous and the mundane, the dreadful and the ridiculous in a novel of imagination and skill . . . The magic, like the mist above this sodden village, seems right for a story about spiritual and sensual awakening'   *Financial Times*

'This is a shrewd and funny book, built on intelligence and compassion. It reminds us that one of the most telling reasons for the revival of the fairy story is an old one. In a hard world, it offers our best chance of a happy ending'
                    London Review of Books

'*Fludd* is a quaint and lovely novel . . . It doesn't only believe in miracles; it believes in happy endings'
                    NICCI GERRARD, *New Statesman*

'The message of Hilary Mantel's excellent and ambitious novel is that the human form of alchemy is perfectly possible; all one needs is love'
                    PAUL PICKERING, *Sunday Times*

By the same author

Wolf Hall
Beyond Black
Every Day is Mother's Day
Vacant Possession
Eight Months on Ghazzah Street
A Place of Greater Safety
A Change of Climate
An Experiment in Love
The Giant, O'Brien
Learning to Talk

NON-FICTION
Giving Up the Ghost

HILARY MANTEL

Fludd

FOURTH ESTATE · London

Fourth Estate
An imprint of HarperCollins*Publishers*
77–85 Fulham Palace Road
Hammersmith
London W6 8JB

This edition published by Fourth Estate 2010

1

First published by Viking 1989
Published in paperback by Harper Perennial 2005

PS™ is a trademark of HarperCollins*Publishers* Ltd

A catalogue record for this book is
available from the British Library

ISBN 978-0-00-717289-4

Printed and bound in Great Britain by
Clays Ltd, St Ives plc

Mixed Sources

Product group from well-managed
forests and other controlled sources
www.fsc.org Cert no. SW-COC-1806
© 1996 Forest Stewardship Council

FSC

FSC is a non-profit international organisation established to promote the
responsible management of the world's forests. Products carrying the FSC
label are independently certified to assure consumers that they come
from forests that are managed to meet the social, economic and
ecological needs of present and future generations.

Find out more about HarperCollins and the environment at
www.harpercollins.co.uk/green

For Anne Ostrowska

Note

The Church in this story bears some but not much resemblance to the Roman Catholic Church in the real world, c. 1956. The village of Fetherhoughton is not to be found on a map.

The real Fludd (1574–1637) was a physician, scholar and alchemist. In alchemy, everything has a literal and factual description, and in addition a description that is symbolic and fantastical.

You are familiar, no doubt, with Sebastiano del Piombo's huge painting *The Raising of Lazarus*, which hangs in the National Gallery in London, having been purchased in the last century from the Angerstein collection. Against a background of water, arched bridges and a hot blue sky, a crowd of people – presumably the neighbours – cluster about the risen man. Lazarus has turned rather yellow in death, but he is a muscular, well-set-up type. His grave-clothes are draped like a towel over his head, and people lean towards him solicitously, and seem to confer; what he most resembles is a boxer in his corner. The expressions of those around are puzzled, mildly censorious. Here – in the very act of extricating his right leg from a knot of the shroud – one feels his troubles are about to begin again. A woman – Mary, or maybe Martha – is whispering behind her hand. Christ points to the revenant, and holds up his other hand, fingers outstretched: so many rounds down, five to go.

Chapter One

On Wednesday the bishop came in person. He was a modern prelate, brisk and plump in his rimless glasses, and he liked nothing better than to tear around the diocese in his big black car.

He had taken the precaution – advisable in the circumstances – of announcing himself two hours before his arrival. The telephone bell, ringing in the hall of the parish priest's house, had in itself a muted ecclesiastical tone. Miss Dempsey heard it as she was coming from the kitchen. She stood looking at the telephone for a moment, and then approached it gingerly, walking on the balls of her feet. She lifted the receiver as if it were hot. Her head on one side, holding the earpiece well away from her cheek, she listened to the message given by the bishop's secretary. 'Yes My Lord,' she murmured, though in retrospect she knew that the secretary did not merit this. 'The bishop and his sycophants', Father Angwin always said; Miss Dempsey supposed they were a kind of deacon. Holding the receiver in her fingertips, she replaced it with great care. She stood in the dim passageway, for a moment, thinking, and bowed her head momentarily, as if she had heard the Holy Name of Jesus. Then she went to the foot of the stairs and bellowed up them: 'Father Angwin, Father Angwin, get yourself up and dressed, the bishop will be upon us before eleven o'clock.'

*

Miss Dempsey went back into the kitchen, and switched on the electric light. It was not a morning when the light made a great deal of difference; the summer, a thick grey blanket, had pinned itself to the windows. Miss Dempsey heard the incessant drip, drip, drip from the branches and leaves outside, and a more urgent metallic drip, pit-pat, pit-pat; it was the guttering. Her figure moved, the electric light behind it, over the dull green wall; immense hands floated towards the kettle; as in a thick sea, her limbs swam for the range. Upstairs, the priest beat his shoe along the floor, and pretended to be coming.

Ten minutes later he had got himself up; she heard the creak of the floorboards above, the gurgle of water from the washbasin, his feet on the stairs. He sighed as he came down the hallway, his solitary morning sigh. Suddenly he was behind her, hovering: 'Agnes, have you something for my stomach?'

'I daresay,' she said. He knew where the salts were kept; but she must get it for him, as if she were his mother. 'Were there many at seven o'clock Mass?'

'It's funny you should ask,' Father said, just as if she did not ask it every morning. 'There were a few old Children of Mary, along with the usual derelicts. It wouldn't be some special feast of theirs, would it? Walpurgisnacht?'

'I don't know what you mean, Father. I'm a Children of Mary myself, as you perfectly well know, and I've not heard of anything.' She looked aggrieved. 'Were they wearing their cloaks and all?'

'No, they were in mufti, just their usual horseblankets.'

Miss Dempsey brought the teapot to the table. 'You ought not to make mock of the Sodalities, Father.'

'I wonder if something has got out about the bishop coming? Some intelligence of a subterranean variety? Am I to have bacon, Agnes?'

'Not with your stomach in its present state.'

Miss Dempsey poured from the pot, a thick brown gurgling stream, adding to the noise: the dripping trees, the wind in the chimneys.

'And another thing,' he said. 'McEvoy was there.' Father Angwin hunched himself over the table. He warmed his hands around his cup. When he said the name of McEvoy, a shadow crossed his face, and hovered about his jaw, so that Miss Dempsey, who was given to imagination, thought for a moment she had seen what he would look like when he was eighty years old.

'Oh yes,' she said, 'and did he want something?'

'No.'

'I wonder why you mention him then?'

'Dear Agnes, give me some peace. Go and let me compose myself for His Corpulence. What does he want, do you think? What's he after this time?'

Agnes went out, a duster in her hand, her face full of complaints. Whatever he had meant about subterranean intelligence, surely he was not accusing her? Nobody but the bishop himself, forming the intention in his deep heart, had known he meant to visit – except perhaps the sycophants might have known. Therefore she, Miss Dempsey, could not know, therefore she could not hint, divulge, reveal, to the Children of Mary or anyone else in the parish. Had she known, she might have mentioned it. Might – if she had thought that anyone needed to know. She herself was the judge of what anyone needed to know. For Miss Dempsey occupied a special mediatory position, between church, convent and everyone else. To acquire information was her positive duty, and then what she did with it was a matter for her judgement and experience. Miss Dempsey would have eavesdropped on the confessional, if she could; she had often wondered how she might manage it.

Left at the breakfast table, Father Angwin stared into his teacup, and shifted it about. Miss Dempsey had not mastered the use of a strainer. Nothing in particular could be seen in the leaves, but for a moment Father Angwin thought that someone had come into the room behind him. He lifted his face, as he did in conversation, but there was no one there. 'Come in, whoever you are,' he said. 'Have some stewed tea.' Father Angwin was a foxy man, with his dead-leaf-colour eyes and hair; head tilted, he sniffed the wind, and shied away from what he detected. Somewhere else in the house, a door slammed.

Consider Agnes Dempsey: duster in hand, whisking it over the dustless bureau. In recent years her face had fallen softly, like a piece of light cotton folding into a box. Her neck too fell in floury, scalloped folds, to where her clothing cut off the view. Her eyes were round, child-like, bright blue, their air of surprise compounded by her invisible eyebrows and her hair, a faded gold streaked with grey, which sprang up from her hairline as if crackling with static. She had pleated skirts, and short bottle-shaped legs, and pastel twin-sets to cover the gentle twin hummocks of her bosom. Her mouth was small and pale and indiscernible, made to ingest the food she liked: Eccles cakes, vanilla slices, miniature chocolate Swiss rolls that came wrapped in red-and-silver foil. It was her habit to peel off the foil carefully, fold it as thin as a pencil, twist it into a ring, and pop it on her wedding finger. Then she would hold out both hands – fingers bloodless and slightly bent by incipient arthritis – and appraise them, a frown of concentration appearing as a single vertical line at the inner corner of her left eyebrow. Then she would rest her hand on her knee for a little; then remove the ring, intact, and throw it on to the fire. This was Miss Dempsey's private habit, which no one had ever seen. Above her upper lip, on the right-hand side, she had a small flat wart, colourless as her mouth itself. It was hard for her not to touch it. She was afraid of cancer.

*

By the time the bishop came bustling in, Father Angwin had got over his hangover. He sat in the parlour, with his neat ingratiating smile. 'Father Angwin, Father Angwin,' the bishop said, crossing the room, and taking him in a grip; hand squeezing upper arm, hand pumping hand, quite beside himself with joviality, and yet those episcopal bifocals glinting and swimming with suspicion, and the episcopal head turning, turning from side to side, like a mechanical toy that you shoot for at a fair.

'Tea,' Father Angwin said.

'No time for tea,' said the bishop. He took up a stance on the hearthrug. 'I've come to talk to you on the subject of uniting all right-thinking people in the family of God,' he said. 'Now then, now then, Father Angwin. I'm expecting trouble from you.'

'Are you going to sit, or what?' Father Angwin asked him diffidently.

The bishop clasped his pink hands before him. He looked severely at the priest, and swayed a little on the spot. 'The next decade, Father Angwin, is the decade of unity. The decade of gathering-in. The decade of Christ's human family. The decade of the Christian community in communion with itself.' Agnes Dempsey came in with a tray. 'Oh, since you've brought it,' the bishop said.

When Miss Dempsey had left the room – her knees had become stiff, owing to the wet weather, and she was obliged to take her time – Father Angwin said, 'Do you mean the decade of burying the hatchet, by any small chance?'

'The decade of reconciliation,' the bishop said, 'the decade of amity, the decade of coexistence and the decade of the many-in-one.'

'You're talking like a person right outside my experience,' Father Angwin said.

'The ecumenical spirit,' the bishop said. 'Don't you feel it in the breeze? Don't you feel it wafted to you on the prayers of a million Christian souls?'

'I feel it breathing on my neck.'

'Am I ahead of my time, or what?' the bishop asked. 'Or is it you, Father Angwin, closing your ears and deaf to the wind of change? And you might pour the tea, for I can't abide tea stewed.'

When Father Angwin had poured the tea, the bishop picked up his cup, and jiggled it in his hand, and took a scalding gulp. Standing before the fireplace, he turned his toes out more widely, and placed his superfluous arm behind his back, and breathed in a noticeable way.

'Exasperated,' Father Angwin said, speaking in a low voice, but not to himself. 'Exasperated with me. Tell me, is that tea hot enough? Good enough? Whisky in it?' He raised his voice. 'I hardly understand you at all.'

'Well,' said the bishop, 'have you heard of the vernacular Mass? Have you thought of it? I think of it. I think of it constantly. There are men in Rome who think of it.'

Father shook his head. 'I couldn't be part of that.'

'No choice, my dear man, no choice; in five years, mark my words, or a little more than five . . .'

Father Angwin looked up. 'Do you mean,' he said, 'that they could understand what we were saying?'

'Exactly the point.'

'Pernicious,' Father muttered audibly. 'Arrant nonsense.' Then, louder, 'I can well understand if you think that Latin's too good for them. But the problem I have here is their little grasp of the English language, do you see?'

'I take account of that,' the bishop said. 'The people of Fetherhoughton are not on a high level. I would not claim that they were.'

'Then what am I to do?'

'Everything conspires to improve them, Father. I will not refer to council housing, as I know it is a sore point in this district . . .'

'*Requiescant in pace*,' Father murmured.

'. . . but have they not free spectacles? Free teeth? In the times we live in, Father Angwin, everything that can be done to improve their material welfare shall be done, and it is for you to think of improving them in the spiritual line. Now, I have some hints and tips for you, which you will kindly accept from me.'

'I don't see why I should,' Father Angwin said, quite loudly enough to be heard, 'when you are such an old fool. I don't see why I can't be a Pope in my own domain.' He looked up. 'Consider me at your disposal.'

The bishop stared; it was a pebbly stare. He pursed his lips and said nothing till he had drunk a second cup. Then, 'I want to look at the church.'

At this early point, the topography of the village of Fetherhoughton may repay consideration. So may the manners, customs and dress of its inhabitants.

The village lay in moorland, which ringed it on three sides. The surrounding hills, from the village streets, looked like the hunched and bristling back of a sleeping dog. Let sleeping dogs lie, was the attitude of the people; for they hated nature. They turned their faces in the fourth direction, to the road and the railway that led them to the black heart of the industrial north: to Manchester, to Wigan, to Liverpool. They were not townspeople; they had none of their curiosity. They were not country people; they could tell a cow from a sheep, but it was not their business. Cotton was their business, and had been for nearly a century. There were three mills, but there were no clogs and shawls; there was nothing picturesque.

In summer the moorland looked black. Tiny distant figures swarmed over the hummocks and hills; they were Water Board men, Forestry Commission. In the folds of the hills there were pewter-coloured reservoirs, hidden from sight. The first event of autumn was the snowfall that blocked the pass that led through the moors to Yorkshire; this was generally accounted a good thing. All winter the snow lay on the hills. By April it had flaked off into scaly patches. Only in the warmest May would it seem to vanish entirely.

The people of Fetherhoughton kept their eyes averted from the moors with a singular effort of will. They did not talk about them. Someone – it was the mark of the outsider – might find a wild dignity and grandeur in the landscape. The Fetherhoughtonians did not look at the landscape at all. They were not Emily Brontë, nor were they paid to be, and the very suggestion that the Brontë-like matter was to hand was enough to make them close their minds and occupy their eyes with their shoelaces. The moors were the vast cemetery of their imaginations. Later, there were notorious murders in the vicinity, and real bodies were buried there.

The main street of Fetherhoughton was known to the inhabitants as Upstreet: 'I am going Upstreet,' they would say, 'to the Co-op drapers.' It was not unprosperous. Behind window displays of tinned salmon, grocers stood ready at their bacon slicers. Besides the Co-op draper, the Co-op general store, the Co-op butcher, the Co-op shoe shop and the Co-op baker, there was Madame Hilda, Modes; and there was a hairdresser, who took the young women into private cubicles, segregated them with plastic curtains, and gave them Permanent Waves. There was no bookshop, nor anything of that sort. But there was a public library, and a war memorial.

Off Upstreet ran other winding streets with gradients of one in four, lined by terraced houses built in the local stone; they had been put up by the mill-owners towards the end of the last century, and rented out to the hands. Their front doors opened straight on to the pavement. There were two rooms downstairs, of which the sitting room was referred to as the House; so that in the unlikely event of anyone from Fetherhoughton explaining their conduct in any way, they might say, 'I cleaned miyoopstairs this morning, this afternoon I am bound fert clean the House.'

The speech of the Fetherhoughtonians is not easy to reproduce. The endeavour is false and futile. One misses the solemnity, the archaic formality of the Fetherhoughtonian dialect. It was a mode of speech, Father Angwin believed, that had come adrift from the language around it. Some current had caught them unawares, and washed the Fetherhoughtonians far from the navigable reaches of plain English; and there they drifted and bobbed on waters of their own, up the creek without a paddle.

But this is a digression, and in those houses there was no scope to digress. In the House there would be a coal fire, no heating in any other room, though there might be a single-bar electric fire kept, to be used in some ill-defined emergency. In the kitchen, a deep sink and a cold-water tap, and a very steep staircase, rising to the first floor. Two bedrooms, a garret: outside, a cobbled yard shared between some ten houses. A row of coalsheds, and a row of lavatories: to each house its own coalshed, but lavatories one between two. These were the usual domestic arrangements in Fetherhoughton and the surrounding districts.

Consider the women of Fetherhoughton, as a stranger might see them; a stranger might have the opportunity, because while the men were shut away in the mills the women liked to stand on their doorsteps. This standing was what they did. Recreational pursuits were for men: football, billiards, keeping hens. Treats were doled out to men, as a reward for good behaviour: cigarettes, beer at the Arundel Arms. Religion, and the public library, were for children. Women only talked. They analysed motive, discussed the serious business, carried life forward. Between the schoolroom and their present state came the weaving sheds; deafened by the noise of the machines, they spoke too loudly now, their voices scattering through the gritty streets like the cries of displaced gulls.

Treeless streets, where the wind blows.

Consider their outdoor (not doorstep) dress. They wore plastic raincoats of a thick, viscous green, impermeable, like alien skins. Should it chance not to rain, the women rolled these raincoats up and left them about the house, where they appeared like reptiles from the Amazon, momentarily coiled in slumber.

For shoes, the women wore bedroom slippers in the form of bootees, with a big zip up the middle. When they went outdoors they put on a stouter version of the same shoe in a tough dark brown suede. Their legs rose like tubes, only an inch or so exposed beneath the hems of their big winter coats.

The younger women had different bedroom slippers, which relatives gave each other every Christmas. They were dish-shaped, each with a thick ruff of pink or blue nylon fur. At first the soles of these slippers were as hard and shiny as glass; it took a week of wear before they bent and gave under the foot, and during that week their wearer would often look down on them with pride, with a guilty sense of luxury, as the nylon fur tickled her ankles. But gradually the fur lost its bounce and spring, and crumbs fell into it; by February its fibres were matted together with chip fat.

From the doorsteps the women stared at passers-by, and laughed. They knew a joke, when it was pointed out to them, but for the most part their entertainment lay in the discernment of physical peculiarities in those around them. They lived in hope of seeing a passer-by with a hunchback, knock knees or a hare lip. They did not think that it was cruel to mock the afflicted, they thought it was perfectly natural; they were sentimental but pitiless, very scathing and unforgiving about any aberration, deviation, eccentricity or piece of originality. There was a spirit abroad in the village that discriminated so thoroughly against pretension that it also discriminated against ambition, even against literacy.

Off Upstreet was Church Street, another steep hill; it was unpopulated, lined with ancient hedgerows, smoke and dust forming a perpetual ash-like deposit on the leaves. Church Street petered out at its summit into a wide track, muddy and stony, which in Fetherhoughton was known as the carriage-drive. Perhaps sometime in the last century a carriage had driven up it, conveying some pious person; the drive went nowhere except to the village school, to the convent and to the Church of St Thomas Aquinas. From the carriage-drive, footpaths led to the hamlet of Netherhoughton, and the moors.

Atop one of the smaller village streets sat a Methodist chapel, square and red, and about it was its cemetery, where chapel-going people came to early graves. There were a few Protestants sprinkled through the terraced rows; each yard might have some. The Protestants' houses did not have, pinned to the door of the cupboard in the sitting room, a coloured picture of the Pontiff with a calendar beneath; but otherwise, their houses were not readily distinguishable.

And yet the Protestants were quite different, in the eyes of their neighbours. They were guilty of culpable ignorance. They refused to take on board the precepts of the True Faith. They knew that St Thomas Aquinas was there, but they refused to go in it. They refused to turn over their children to Mother Perpetua for a good Catholic education, and preferred to send them on a bus to a school in another village.

Mother Perpetua would tell the children, with her famous, dangerously sweet smile: 'We have no objection to Protestants worshipping God in their own way. But we Catholics prefer to worship Him in his.'

The Protestants were damned, of course, by reason of this culpable ignorance. They would roast in hell. A span of seventy years, to ride bicycles in the steep streets, to get married, to eat bread and dripping: then bronchitis, pneumonia, a broken hip: then the minister calls, and the florist does a wreath: then devils will tear their flesh with pincers.

It is a most neighbourly thought.

The Church of St Thomas Aquinas was a massive building; its walls were plastered by deposits of soot and grease, so that their original grey was black. It stood on a kind of pimple of higher ground, and this fact occasioned little flights of stone steps and cobbled ramps, slippery and mossy underfoot; clustering at the base of the tower, they looked like household terriers running at the feet of some dangerous, dirty tramp.

The Church was in fact less than a hundred years old; it had been built when the Irish came to Fetherhoughton to work in the three cotton mills. But someone had briefed its architect to make it look as if it had always stood there. In those poor, troubled days it was an understandable wish, and the architect had a sense of history; it was a Shakespearian sense of history, with a grand contempt of the pitfalls of anachronism. Last Wednesday and the Battle of Bosworth are all one; the past is the past, and Mrs O'Toole, buried last Wednesday, is neck and neck with King Richard in the hurtle to eternity. This was – it must have been – the architect's view. From the Romans to the Hanoverians, it was all the same to him; they wore, no doubt, leather jerkins and iron crowns; they burned witches; their buildings were stone and quaint and cold, their windows were not as our windows; they slapped their thighs and said prithee. Only such a vision could have commanded into being the music-hall medievalism of St Thomas Aquinas.

The architect had begun in a vaguely Gothic way and ended with something Saxon and brutal. There was a tower at the west end, without spire or pinnacles, but furnished with battlements. The porch had stone benches, and a plain holy-water stoup, and malodorous matting that was beaten thin by scuffling feet – matting that was always sodden, and might have been composed of some thirsty vegetable matter.

The doorway had a round arch of a Norman persuasion, but no recessed arches, no little shafts, no ornament, not so much as a lozenge, a zigzag, a chevron; stern had been the mood the day that doorway was designed, and the door itself was strapped and hinged in a manner that put one in mind of siege warfare and starvation and a populace reduced to eating its rats.

Inside the church, in the pit-like gloom, there was a deep font, without ornament, with a single plain shaft, and big enough to cope with a multiple birth, or dip a sheep. There was a west gallery for the organ, with a patch of deeper blackness beneath it; the gallery itself, though you would not know until you had swum into that blackness, was reached by a low little doorway with junior siege-hinges, and a treacherous spiral staircase, with risers a foot deep. There were two side chapels, two aisles, and it was in the arcades that the architect's derangement was most evident, for the arches were round or pointed, seemingly as a consequence of some spur-of-the-moment decision, and as one blundered through the nave, the confusion of style gave the church a misleadingly heroic air, as if it had been built, like one of the great European cathedrals, in successive campaigns a hundred years apart. The shafts of the columns were squat and massive cylinders, made of a greyish, finely pitted stone, and their uncarved capitals resembled packing cases.

The lancet windows were grouped two by two, and surmounted by grudging tracery, here a circle, here a quatrefoil, here a dagger trefoil. In each of the lights stood a glass saint, bearing his name on an unfurling scroll, each scroll inscribed in an unreadable Germanic black-letter; the faces of these glass saints were identical, their expressions were all alike. The glass itself was of a mill-town sort; there was a light-refusing, industrial quality about its thick texture, and its colours were blatant and vile: a traffic-light green, a sugar-bag blue and the dull but acidic red of cheap strawberry jam.

There were stone flags underfoot, and the long benches were varnished with a treacly red stain; the doors to the single confessional were low and latched, like the doors to a coalshed.

Father Angwin and the bishop came out through the draughty vaulted passage from the sacristy, and emerged by the Lady chapel in the north aisle. They looked about; not that it profited them. In all, St Thomas Aquinas was as dark as Notre-Dame and resembled it in one other alarming particular – that at any given moment, standing in one part, you lost all sense of what might be happening in another. You could not see the roof, although you had – in St Thomas Aquinas – an uneasy, crawling feeling about it, that it might not be so far above your head at all, and that it might lower itself a little from time to time, just that little inch or so that betrayed its ambition to unite, one winter's day, with the stone flags, and freeze into a solid block of unwrought masonry, with the worshippers between. The church's inner spaces were aggregations of darkness, with channels of thicker darkness between. There were plaster saints – which the bishop now surveyed as best he might – and before most of them, in severe iron racks that looked like the bars of a beast-house, devotional candles burned; yet it was a lightless burning, like marsh-gas, a flickering in an unfelt, breathless wind. There were draughts, it was true, which followed each worshipper like a bad reputation, which dabbed at their ankles and climbed into their clothes, as cats do with people who do not like them. But when the church was empty the draughts lay quiet, only whistling from time to time about the floor; and the candle flames rose up towards the roof, straight and thin as dressmaker's pins.

'These statues,' said the bishop. 'Have you a pocket torch?' Father Angwin did not reply. 'Then give me a tour,' the bishop demanded. 'Start here. I cannot identify this fellow. Is he a Negro?'

'Not really. He's been painted. A lot of them have. That's St Dunstan. Don't you see his tongs?'

'What has he got tongs for?' the bishop asked rudely. He stared at the saint in a hostile way, his paunch thrust out.

'He was working at his forge when the devil came to tempt him, and the saint seized his nose with red-hot pincers.'

'I wonder what sort of temptations you might get while working at a forge.' The bishop peered into the darkness. 'There are a lot of them, Father. You have more statues than any church in the diocese.' He passed on down the aisle. 'How did you get them? Where did they come from?'

'They were here before my time. They've always been here.'

'You know that is impossible. They were someone's decision. Who is this woman with the pliers? This place is like an ironmonger's shop.'

'That's Apollonia. The Romans pulled her teeth out. She's the patron saint of dentists.' Father Angwin looked up into the martyr's downturned, expressionless face. He stooped and took a candle from the wooden box at the statue's foot, and lit it from the solitary flame that burned below Dunstan. He carried it back with care, and fitted it into one of Apollonia's empty candle-holders. 'Nobody bothers with her. They don't go in for dentistry here. Their teeth fall out quite early in life, and they find it a relief.'

'Pass on,' said the bishop.

'Here are my four Church Fathers. You will see St Gregory in his Papal tiara.'

'I cannot see anything.'

'You must take my word for it. And St Augustine, holding a heart, you see, pierced with an arrow. And the other Fathers here, St Jerome with his little lion.'

'It really is a very small beast.' The bishop leant forward, put himself nose to nose with it. 'Not realistic at all.'

Father Angwin put his hand on the lion's arched mane,

and traced the length of its stone back with his forefinger. 'I like him the best of all the Fathers. I think of him in the desert with his wild eyes and his bare hermit's knees.'

'Who's left?' said the bishop. 'Ambrose. Ambrose with his hive.'

'St Beehive, the children call him. Similarly it was mentioned in the parish some two generations back that Augustine was the Bishop of Hippo, and since then I am afraid that there has been a great deal of confusion among the juveniles, passed on carefully, you see, by their parents.'

The bishop made a little growl, deep in his throat. Father Angwin had the feeling that he had somehow played into the bishop's hands; that the bishop would think that it mattered, if they were confused.

'Can it matter?' he said quickly. 'Look at St Agatha here, poor Christian soul, carrying her breasts on a dish. Why is she the patron saint of bellfounders? Because a little mistake was made, with the shape; you can understand it. Why do we bless bread in a dish on 5 February? Because as well as looking like bells they look like bread rolls. It is a harmless mistake. It is more decent than the truth. It is less cruel.'

They had passed by now almost to the back of the church, and in the north aisle, opposite them, there were more saints; St Bartholomew clutched the knife with which he had been flayed, St Cecilia her portable organ. A Virgin, with the foolish expression imparted by a sickly smile and a chipped nose, held her blue arms out stiffly under her drapery; and St Theresa, the Little Flower, glowered from beneath her wreath of roses.

The bishop crossed the church, and looked up into the Carmelite's face, and tapped her foot. 'I make exceptions, Father,' he said. 'Our boys in the trenches of Flanders addressed their prayers through the Little Flower, and some of those who did so were I daresay not Catholic at all. There are saints for our time, Father, and this one here is a shining example to all Catholic womanhood. Perhaps this one may stay. I will give it consideration.'

'Stay?' the priest said. 'Where are they going?'

'Out,' said the bishop succinctly. 'And where, I care not. Somehow, Father Angwin, I shall drag you and your church and your parishioners into the 1950s, where we all quite firmly belong. I cannot have this posturing, Father, I cannot have this idolatry.'

'But they are not idols. They are just statues. They are just representations.'

'And if I were to walk out on to the street, Father, and I were to lay hold of one of your parishioners, do you think he would be able to distinguish, to my satisfaction, between that honour and reverence that we give the saints and that worship that belongs to God?'

'Windbag,' said Father Angwin. 'Dechristianizer. Saladin.' He pitched his voice up. 'It isn't what you think. But the people here are very deficient in the power of prayer. They are simple people. I am a simple man myself.'

'I am aware of that,' the bishop said.

'The saints have their attributes. They have their areas of interest. A congregation latches on to them.'

'They must latch off,' said the bishop brutally. 'I won't have it. These are to go.'

As he passed Michael the Archangel, Father Angwin looked up and saw the scales in which that saint weighs human souls, and he dropped his eyes to Michael's foot: a bare, muscled, claw-like foot, that had sometimes seemed to him like the foot of an ape. He passed under the gallery, into the thicker, velvet blackness where St Thomas himself, the Angelic Doctor, stood central and square on his plinth, his stone gaze on the high altar, and the star that he held in his fine hands shedding lightless rays into the greater dark.

Chapter Two

When they returned to the house, the bishop was boisterous and offensive. He wanted more tea, and biscuits too. 'I won't dispute it,' he said. 'I won't dispute it any more. Your congregation have superstitions that would disgrace Sicilian peasants.'

'But I am afraid,' Father Angwin said, 'that if you take away the statues, and next the Latin, next the feast days, the fast days, the vestments —'

'I said nothing about this, did I?'

'I can see the future. They won't come any more. Why should they? Why should they come to church? They might as well be out in the street.'

'We are not here for frills and baubles, Father,' said the bishop. 'We are not here for fripperies. We are here for Christian witness.'

'Rubbish,' Father said. 'These people aren't Christians. These people are heathens and Catholics.'

When Agnes Dempsey came in with the Nice biscuits she could see that Father Angwin was in a poor state, quivering and sweating and passing his hand over his forehead. She hung about in the corridor, to catch what she could.

'Well, come now,' the bishop said. She could hear that he was alarmed. 'Don't take on so. I'm not saying you may not have an image. I'm not saying that you may not have a statue at all. I'm saying we must make an accommodation to the times in which we live.'

'I don't see why,' Father said, adding audibly, 'you fat fool.'

'Are you quite well?' the bishop said. 'You keep talking in different voices. Insulting me.'

'If the truth insults you.'

'Never mind,' said the bishop. 'I am of robust character. But I think, Father Angwin, that you must have an assistant. Some young chap, as strong as myself. It seems to me you know next to nothing of the tide of the times. Do you look at television?' Father Angwin shook his head. 'You don't possess a receiving set,' said the bishop. 'You should, you know. Broadcasting is our greatest asset, wisely used. Why, I cannot count the good that has been done in the Republic, in helping the denominations understand each other, by Rumble and Carty's "Radio Replies". Depend upon it, Father, that's the future.' The bishop smote the mantelpiece, like Moses striking the rock.

Father Angwin surveyed him. Irish as he was, where had he got that Anglo complexion, rosy and cyanosed by turn? At a public school, surely, a minor English public school. If it had stood to Father Angwin, the bishop would not have been educated, or at least not in that way. He needed to know who was Galileo, and to chant in choir for a few hours at a time. The lives of the saints would have been enough for him, and the movement of the spheres, and a touch of practical wisdom on dairy farming or some such, that was useful to a pastoral economy.

All this he voiced to the bishop; the bishop stared. Outside the door Miss Dempsey stood with her blue eyes growing brighter, sucking one finger like a child who has burnt it on the stove. She heard footsteps above, in the passage, in the bedroom. It is ghosts, she thought, walking on my mopping. Angelic doctors, virgin martyrs. Doors slammed overhead.

The rain had stopped. Silence crept through the house. The bishop was a modern man, no patience with scruples, no time for the ancient byways of faith; and what can you do, against a modern man? When Father Angwin spoke again, the note of contention had gone from his voice; fatigue replaced it. 'Those statues are as tall as men,' he said.

'Get help,' said the bishop. 'You have plenty of help. Get the parishioners to assist. Get the Men's Fellowship on to it.'

'Where am I to put them? I can't break them up.'

'Well, agreed. It wouldn't be wholly decent. Stack them in your garage. Why don't you do that?'

'What about my vehicle?'

'What? Is that the thing, outside?'

'My motor car,' Father said.

'That heap of junk? Why not expose it to the elements?'

'It's true,' Father Angwin said humbly, 'it's a worthless car. You can see the road through the floor as you drive.'

'I can remember,' the bishop said abrasively, 'when chaps got about on bicycles.'

Chaps, Father thought. Chaps is it, now? 'You couldn't go to Netherhoughton on a bicycle,' he said. 'They'd knock you off it.'

'Good heavens,' the bishop said. He looked over his shoulder, being imperfectly certain of the geography of this most northerly outpost of the diocese. 'Are they Orangemen up there?'

'They have an Orange Lodge. They are all in it, Catholics too. They have firework parties in Netherhoughton. Oxroasts. They play football with human heads.'

'At some point you exaggerate,' the bishop said. 'I am not sure at which.'

'Would you care to make a pastoral visit?'

'Indeed not,' said the bishop. 'I have pressing matters. I must be getting back. You may keep Thomas Aquinas, St Theresa the Little Flower and the Holy Virgin herself, only try if you can to get her nose repaired.'

Miss Dempsey moved away from the door. The bishop came out into the hall and gave her a piercing look. She wiped her hands nervously on her pinny and knelt on the floor. 'May I kiss the ring, M' lud?'

'Oh, get away, woman. Get into the kitchen. Contribute something practical, will you?'

'The bishop cannot abide the piety of the ignorant,' Father Angwin said.

Miss Dempsey got painfully to her feet. Two strides carried the bishop through the hall, a thrust of his arms carried him into his cape, and he threw open the front door, tussling on the path with the damp, windy day. 'Summer's over,' he observed. 'Not that you see much of it at this end of the diocese.'

'Allow me to attend you into your princely vehicle,' Father Angwin said. He had bowed his shoulders, and adopted a servile tone.

'That will do,' the bishop said. He eased himself into the driver's seat, grunting a little. He knew that Angwin was mad, but he did not want a scandal in the diocese. 'I shall visit you again,' he said, 'when you least expect it. To see that everything has been done.'

'Okey-dokey,' Father Angwin said. 'I'll prepare the boiling oil for you.'

The bishop roared away, with a clashing and meshing of gears; around the next bend the schoolchildren brought him to a halt, processing out of the gate to the Nissen hut for their dinners. The bishop put his fist on his horn and blew out two long blasts at the mites, scattering them into the ditch. They crawled out and stared after him, wet leaves sticking to their bare knees.

In Father Angwin's parlour the tinny little mantel-clock struck twelve. 'Too late,' Agnes Dempsey said, in a discouraged tone. 'Only, Father, I was thinking to cheer you up. If you pray to St Anne before twelve o'clock on a Wednesday, you'll get a pleasant surprise before the end of the week.'

Father Angwin shook his head. 'Tuesday, Agnes my lamb. Not Wednesday. We have to be exact in these matters.'

Her invisible eyebrows rose a fraction. 'So that's why it has never worked. But there's another thing, Father – I must alert you. I can hear a person walking about upstairs, when nobody is there.'

Nervously, she put her hand up to her mouth, and touched the pale flat wart.

'Yes, it happens,' Father Angwin said. He sat on a hard chair at the dining table, huddled into himself, his rust-coloured head bowed. 'I often think it is myself.'

'But you are here.'

'At this moment, yes. Perhaps it is a forerunner. Someone who is to come.'

'The Lord?' Miss Dempsey asked wildly.

'The curate. I am threatened with a curate. What a very extraordinary curate that would be ... a walker without feet, a melter through walls. But no. Probably not.' He forced himself to sit up straighter. 'I expect the bishop will send some ordinary spy. Just with ordinary powers.'

'A sycophant.'

'Just so.'

'What will you do with the statues, Father? You know the garage has not got a roof, in the proper meaning of the word. They would be exposed to the damp. They would get mould. It hardly seems right.'

'You think we should treat them with reverence, Agnes. You think they are not just lumps of paint and plaster.'

'All my life,' Agnes said impressively, 'all my life, Father, I have known those statues. I cannot think how we will find our way around the church without them. It will be like some big filthy barn.'

'Have you any ideas?'

'They could be boarded out. With different people. The Children of Mary would take St Agatha, turn and turn about. We would need a van, mind. She couldn't fit in your car.'

'But they would get tired of her, Agnes. Suppose one of them got a husband? He might not like its presence in the house. And then, you know, people in Fetherhoughton have so little room. I'm afraid it would not be a permanent solution.'

Miss Dempsey looked stubborn. 'They ought to be preserved. In case of a change of bishop.'

'No. I'm afraid they will never be wanted again. We are asking for time to run backwards. The bishop is right about so many things, but I wish he would stick to his politics and keep out of religion.'

'Then what's to be done?' Miss Dempsey put up her hand, and wavered, then touched her wart. 'They're like people, to me. They're like my relatives. I wouldn't put my relatives in a garage.'

'Faith is dead,' Father Angwin said. 'Its time is up. And faith being dead, if we are not to become automatons we must hang on to our superstitions as hard as we may.' He looked up. 'You're quite right, Agnes. It isn't proper to put them in a garage like old lumber, and I'll not farm them out around the parish and have them left on street corners. We'll keep them together. And somewhere we know where they are. We'll bury them. That's what we'll do. We'll bury them in the church grounds.'

'Oh, dear God.' Tears of fright and fury sprang into Agnes's eyes. 'Forgive me Father, but there's something inexpressibly horrible about the idea.'

'I shan't have a service,' Father Angwin said. 'Just an interment.'

You could not say that in Fetherhoughton there was a bush telegraph, for in that place, scoured as it was by Siberian winds, you could not find a bush. Nevertheless, by the time the schoolchildren were released next day for their morning break, everyone had heard of the developments.

St Thomas Aquinas School had been, in their grandparents' time, one long schoolroom; but the rowdyism and ill-behaviour of successive generations had rendered this hugger-mugger sort of education impossible, and now flimsy partitioning divided one age of children from the next. Of course, when the school had been founded, great girls and boys of twelve years old were recognized to have no more need of arithmetic and improving verses, and were launched on the world to begin their adult careers among the textile machines. But now civilization had advanced so far that fifteen-year-olds occupied the Top Class, towering over Mother Perpetua, who was the headmistress, and who was responsible for keeping this Top Class from the excesses of frustrated youth.

And yet it was not youth as we know it, because Youth, elsewhere, was in the process of being invented. A faint intimation of it reached Fetherhoughton; the boys of fifteen slicked their hair greasily over their knobbly foreheads, and sometimes, like people suffering from a nervous disease and beset by uncontrollable tics, they would make claws of their hands and strum them repetitiously across their bellies. Mother Perpetua called it 'imitating skiffle groups'. It was a punishable offence.

These boys were undergrown youths, their faces burnt from kicking footballs into the moorland wind. They were vague and heedless, and their childhoods hung about them. The narrow backs of their necks showed it, and their comic papers, and their sudden indecorous bursts of high spirits – indecorous, because high spirits are a foolish waste in those destined for the chain gang of marriage and the mill.

But in the Big Girls there was no vestige of childhood left. The Big Girls wore cardigans, and at playtime they skulked together in a knot by the wall, their faces moody, spreading scandal. They clasped their arms across their chests, hands hugging woollen upper arms: podgy hands, and low-slung bosoms like their grandmothers. Their cheap clothes were often small for them, and it was this that gave them their indecent womanliness; it was a rule, in the outside world, that girls stopped growing at about this age, but if you had seen the big girls of Fetherhoughton you would say, they will never stop growing, they will devour the world. The school-room chairs creaked under their bottoms; from time to time, nodding forward, swaying, and raucous, rhythmic, terrible, they would laugh: hehr, hehr, hehr.

The girls had learnt nothing; or if they had, they had forgotten it, immediately and as a matter of policy. The school was a House of Detention to them. Many of them suffered poor sight, and had done from their early years; the school nurse came, with letters on cards, and tested their eyes, and the State gave them spectacles. But they would not wear them. 'Men seldom make passes at girls who wear glasses.' But no one will make passes at them anyway. The process by which they will eventually mate and reproduce is invisible and had better remain so. They may as well have their astigmatism corrected, for all the sexual success it will bring them.

While the big girls leant by the wall, and while the big boys with their footballs tacked across the square of asphalt, the juniors of Fetherhoughton, red in tooth and claw, occupied themselves in games of tag, in hopscotch and skip-ping games. Their games were played in a fever of intoler-ance, an agony to those who could not hop or skip; as for tag, it was their habit to pick on some poor child more than usually ragged, or stupid, or scrofulous, and to bawl out his name, and declare you had his 'touch' and must pass it on. Of those not caught up in these games, a number occupied themselves in jumping, time after time, from the low wall that divided the upper level of the playground from the lower; others started fights. The level of disorder, the incidence of injury, was so high, that Mother Perpetua was obliged to segregate the infant class from the rest of the school at playtime, and corral them in a cobbled, evil-smelling yard at the back of the building; it was here, under the shadow of a moss-covered wall some twenty feet in height, that the school had its privies. It will not do to call them lavatories, for there was no provision to wash. To wash would have been thought an affectation.

Above the school the ground banked steeply, towards the convent and the church; below, it fell away to the village. The dismal wooded slopes that flanked the carriage-drive were referred to by local people as 'the terraces'. From the wall at the lower end of the playground, the children looked down on tree-tops; behind the school, above the towering wall that fenced the infants in, they could see the gnarled and homeless and jutting roots of other trees, thrust out from the hillside and growing into air. These terraces were lightless places, without footholds, and it was a peculiarity of their trees that they bore foliage only at the very top; so that below the green canopy there twisted a mile of black branches, like a witch's knitting. Autumn came early; and underfoot, at every season of the year, there was a sunless mulch of dead leaves.

On this particular day, the playground was more than usually animated; the children surged into knots and unravelled themselves again, and streamed wailing across the asphalt, and banked up against the low dividing wall. 'St Hippo', they shouted, and 'St Beehive'; they made their arms into the wings of bombers, and wheeled and dived, and made the snarling whining noise of engines and the crunch of impact and the whoosh of flames.

Mother Perpetua watched them from the school door. She watched for a minute or two, and then with a swift rustle passed back into the shadows, and re-emerged with her cane. She lifted her habit four inches, and thrust out her laced black shoes and strode; then she was amongst the children, arm uplifted, her great deep sleeve falling back to reveal underlayers of black wool. 'In, in, in,' cried Mother Perpetua, 'get in with you, get in.' Her cane rose and fell across the children's fraying jerseys. Howling, they dispersed. A bell rang; mouths agape, they ran into little lines, and sniffled back into their classrooms. Mother Perpetua watched them in, until the playground was empty; a damp wind picked at her skirts. She tucked the cane under her arm, and marched out of the school gates, and up the road to see Father Angwin. As she passed the convent she scanned its windows for signs of life, but could see none; could see nothing to displease her.

Quite unable to grasp her name, the local people had always called her Mother Purpiture; the more irreverent school-children called her Old Ma Purpit, and it was some years since Father Angwin himself had thought of her by any other name. Purpit was a stumpy woman, of middle years – it is not proper to speculate about the exact age of nuns. Her skin was pale and rather spongy, her nose of the fleshy sort; she had a hoarse flirtatious laugh, and with this laugh, a way of flicking a corner of her veil back over her left shoulder; she had tombstone teeth.

Miss Dempsey brought her in, doing the office of a maid, her hands clasped before her at about the bottom button of her twin-set. 'Mother Purpiture,' she announced, grave and respectful. Father Angwin was not reading his breviary, but he at once picked it up, defensively, from the table beside him. Agnes took a little pace back to admit the nun, and stood uneasily fingering her artificial pearls, her mouth turned down at the corners. 'Will you be wanting tea?' she exhaled; and let her eyes travel from side to side. Without an answer, she effaced herself; slid behind Mother Perpetua, and left the room backwards.

Perpetua took a gay little step, arching her instep in the lace-up shoes. 'Ah, but I'm interrupting you,' she said.

I hope Agnes does not bring in tea, Father Angwin thought. I hope she does not take that upon herself. It would be encouraging Purpit. 'Take a seat?' he said. But Purpit continued her dance.

'Can I believe the evidence of my ears?' she asked. 'Is it true that the bishop wants the statues disposed of?'

'It is true.'

'I always thought the church was cluttered. Not that it is for me to say.'

'Not that it is for you to say,' Father Angwin muttered.

Purpit flicked her veil back over her shoulder. 'Do I also hear right? That you mean to bury them? Because what do you want, Father? Do you mean to have the village up here with wreaths? Or do you mean the congregation should just go on as normal and pretend that they are not buried and light their candles round the graves?'

'It is you who say, graves. I have not said any other than "holes". It is not a ceremony. It is not a rite. It is a measure.' Hearing himself say this, Father Angwin found himself consoled a little. 'A measure' gave it distance, gave it dignity, gave it an air of calculation.

'And when do you intend taking this measure?'

'I thought of Saturday. To have the services of the Men's Fellowship.'

'Well, and I can lend you Sister Philomena. A fine strong girl. She can dig. A true daughter of the Irish soil.'

'Oirish', she said; it was her little joke. You cannot expect much of the humour of nuns. Purpit gave her hoarse horse laugh, and flicked her veil again. 'I hear you're threatened with a curate,' she said.

Father Angwin noted her choice of word. He looked up. Between Mother Perpetua's two front teeth, there was a gap; not an uncommon thing, but Father Angwin found that it attracted his eye. He thought of Mother Perpetua as a cannibal; and through that gap, in his imagination, she pulled and sucked the more tender bits of her victims. 'Well, you never know,' the nun said. 'Fresh blood.'

The Saturday following was the day that Father Angwin had marked out for the interment; and he had chosen dusk, to draw a veil of decency over the indecent. The weather had cleared, and the declining sun gold-tipped the battlements; in the damp, moss-scented air, house-martins dipped and wheeled over the presbytery.

The Men's Fellowship, when they were assembled in their ancient and greeny-black suits, wore an aspect of mourning. 'I don't know,' Father Angwin said, 'but would not corduroys have been more suitable?' In all his years in the parish he had not reconciled himself to the strange and hybrid character of the place. He knew in his heart that they were clerks and millhands, that they had no corduroys, no woollen shirts, no rustic boots.

The married men, on the whole, eschewed the Fellowship. They came to church but once a year, and that at Easter or thereabouts; they left such business to their wives. But there were many bachelors in the parish, men of middle years for the most part, desiccated through abstinence and yellow through long devotion; clerics *manqués*, but most of them too humble or stupid to put themselves forward as candidates for ordination. The smell of mould arose from the speckled shoulders of their jackets, and, being hung about with holy medals, they clanked as they walked. Some of them, as he knew from the confessional, practised austerities: meagre diets, the denial of tobacco. He suspected much else: hair shirts, knotted-string scourges. Only supernumerary devotions could kindle their dull eyes. Each lived for the day when he might help an elderly nun across the road, or be nodded to by a monsignor.

The ground had been professionally prepared, for Father Angwin was not about to overtax or overestimate his crew. The gravedigger and his assistant had been called in from the cemetery that St Thomas Aquinas shared with the neighbouring parish; the Fetherhoughtonians did not merit a facility of their own. There had been a discussion (heated) in the church porch, and eventually, and after money had changed hands, the two craftsmen had seen the logic of the priest's case. True, they were not employed to dig holes; it was not their vocation, it did not agree with them. For that he might better have employed, as one of them pointed out, a landscape gardener. But given that the holes were grave-shaped, it might be seen as trespassing on their speciality should he retain some other professional; and the holes need not be so deep as graves, so the work would be easy. They had conceded the point, and excavated the ground behind the garage.

When Father Angwin saw the holes he clasped his arms across his chest, hugging behind his soutane a nameless, floating anxiety; what he saw was a graveyard prepared for some coming massacre or atrocity, and he said to himself, as clever children always say, if God knows our ends, why cannot he prevent them, why is the world so full of malice and cruelty, why did God make it at all and give us free will if he knows already that some of us will destroy ourselves in exercising it? Then he remembered that he did not believe in God, and he went into the church to supervise the removal of the statues from their plinths.

Father Angwin had himself a good knowledge of the principles of levers and pulleys, but it was Sister Philomena who, by example, spurred the Men's Fellowship on to the effort needed. By the time the statues were out of doors, and the men had coiled their ropes and picked up their shovels, the scent of her skin had seeped to them through her heavy black habit, and they edged away, their celibate frames shaken by what they did not understand. She was a big, healthy girl, in her woollen stockings. You were conscious of the smell of soap from her skin, of her eyebrows and of her feet, and of other parts you do not notice on nuns. It was possible to think of her having knees.

Sister Philomena lifted her skirts a fraction to kneel on the damp ground, watching intently as the saints were lowered into the earth. At the last moment she leant forward, and skimmed her rough housewife's hand across the mane of St Jerome's lion; then she eased herself back, settled on her haunches and drew the back of her hand across her eyes.

'I liked him, Father,' she said, looking up. He put out a hand to assist her; she rose smoothly and stood beside him, tipping back her head so that her veil dropped itself over her shoulder into its proper folds. Her hand was warm and steady, and he felt the slow beat of her pulse through the skin.

'You are a good girl,' he said. 'A good girl. I could not have managed. I am too sad.'

Philomena raised her voice to the Men's Fellowship, who were teetering and swaying one-legged, black flamingos, scraping off their shoes. 'You all gentlemen should go to the Nissen hut now. Sister Anthony has got the tea urn out and is baking you some fruit-loaf.'

At this news, the men looked cast down. Sister Anthony, a rotund and beaming figure in her floury apron, was feared throughout the parish.

'Poor old soul,' Father Angwin said. 'She means well. Think of the good sisters, they have to face it every day, breakfast dinner and tea. Do this last one thing for me, lads, and if it is very unpalatable, you must offer it up.'

'There's not more than a handful of grit in it,' Philomena said, 'though possibly more grit than currants. You can offer it up as Father says, make it an occasion of obtaining grace. Say "*Sacred Heart of Jesus, help me to eat this fruit-bread.*"'

'Is that what you say?' Father Angwin asked her. 'I mean, *mutatis mutandis*, with suitable adaptation? For instance, I believe she burns the porridge?'

'*Holy Mary, Mother of God, help me swallow this porridge.* Sister Polycarp suggested we might make a novena to St Michael, the patron saint of grocers, to ask him to guide her a little in the foodstuffs line. We wondered if it was the patron saint of cooks we should apply to, but Sister Polycarp said her problem is more basic than that, it is what she can do with the raw ingredients that God alone knows.'

'And do you all have some pious formula?'

'Oh yes, but we say it under our breath, you know, not to hurt her feelings. Except Mother Perpetua, of course. She gives her a pious rebuke.'

'I'll bet she does.'

'But Sister Anthony is very humble. She never says anything back.'

'Why should she? She has her means of revenge.'

The moon had risen now, a sliver of light over the black terraces. Judd McEvoy, a singular figure in his knitted waistcoat, gave a pat to the earth above St Agatha. 'Judd?' said Father Angwin. 'I did not see you there.'

'Oh, I have been toiling,' Judd McEvoy said. 'Toiling unobtrusively. No reason, Father, why you should remark my presence above the others.'

'No, but I generally do.' Father Angwin turned away. Philomena saw the puzzlement on his face. 'I like to know where you are, Judd,' he remarked, to himself. And louder, 'Are you going to cut along with the others and get your fruit-bread?'

'I shall go directly,' said Judd. 'I should not like to be marked out in any way.' He knocked the earth off his spade, and straightened up. 'I think you may say, Father, that all your saints are safely buried. Shall I take it upon myself to draw up a plan marking the name of each? In case the bishop should change his mind, and wish to reinstate some of them?'

'That will not be necessary.' Father Angwin shifted from foot to foot. 'I myself will remember. I will not be in any doubt.'

'As you please,' McEvoy said. He smiled his cold smile, and put on his hat. 'I will join the others then.'

The Men's Fellowship, edified by the words of the remarkable young nun, were touching their foreheads to Father Angwin and setting off in ones and twos down the drive towards the school. Their murmur arose through the scented evening: *Sacred Heart of Jesus, help me to eat this fruit-bread*. Father Angwin watched them go. McEvoy went with the rest, casting a glance behind him. When finally he rounded the bend by the convent, and was lost to view, Sister Philomena heard the priest let out his breath, and noted the relief on his face.

'Come into the church a moment,' Father Angwin said.

She nodded, and followed him. They entered together, through the deep shadows that had gathered in the porch. A chill struck upwards from the stone floor into their feet. Clods of earth lay in the aisles. 'I will see to this tomorrow,' Philomena said, her tone low and subdued. They looked about. Without the statues the church seemed smaller and meaner, its angles more gracelessly exposed.

'You would think it would be the other way round,' Philomena said, catching his thought. 'That it would look bigger – not that it isn't big enough. Yet I remember when I was a girl and my Aunt Dymphna died, and when we got all the stuff out into the yard, her bed and the chest and all, we went back in to take a last look at it, and the room was like the size of a hen coop. My mother said, dear God, did my sister Dymphna and all her fancy frocks live in this little space?'

'What did she die of?'

'Dymphna? Oh, her lungs. It was a damp place that she lived. On a farm.'

They whispered, as they were speaking of the dead; Philomena bowed her head, and a sharp picture came into the priest's mind, of the decaying thatch of her aunt's cottage, and of chickens, who enjoyed comparatively such liberty, scratching up the sacred soil of Ireland under a sky packed with rain-swollen clouds. It was the day of Dymphna's funeral he was seeing, a coffin being put into a cart. 'I trust she is at peace,' he said.

'I doubt it. She was a byword in her day. She used to go round the cattle fairs and strike up with men. God rest her.'

'You are a curious young woman,' Father Angwin said, looking up at her. 'You have put pictures in my head.'

'I wish you could see the end of this,' Philomena said. 'I feel sad myself, Father. Weighed-upon, somehow. I liked the little lion. Is it true that there is to be a curate?'

'So the bishop tells me. I have heard nothing more from him. I expect the fellow will just turn up.'

'Well, he will be able to see that you have done as you were directed. It is rather poor, what remains.' She walked away from him towards the altar, stopping to genuflect with a thoughtful, slow reverence. 'May I light a candle, Father?'

'You may if you have a match. Otherwise there is nothing to light it from.'

A dim outline in the centre aisle, she reached into the deep pocket of her habit, took out a box of matches, struck one, and picked a new candle from the wooden box beneath the statue of the Virgin. When the wick kindled she shielded the flame with her palm, and held the candle up above her head; the point of light wavered and grew and bathed the statue's face. 'Her nose is chipped.'

'Yes.' Father Angwin spoke from the darkness behind her. 'I wonder if you could see your way to doing anything about it? I am not of an artistic bent.'

'Plasticine,' Philomena said. 'I can get some from the children. Then no doubt we could paint it.'

'Let us go,' Father Angwin said. 'Agnes has cooked some undercut for my supper, and besides, this spectacle is too melancholy.'

'Not more melancholy than the supper that awaits me. I fear it may be the fruit-bread.'

'I should like to ask you to join me,' Father Angwin said, 'on account of the comradeship occasioned by our night's work, but I think I should have to telephone the bishop to ask him for a dispensation of some sort, and no doubt he would have to apply to Rome.'

'I will face the fruit-bread,' Philomena said calmly.

As they left the church, he thought that a hand brushed his arm. Dymphna's bar-parlour laugh came faintly from the terraces; her tipsy, Guinness-sodden breath, stopped by earth these eleven years, filled the summer night.

Chapter Three

Soon after, the school term ended. The mills closed for Wakes Week, and those of the populace who could afford it went to spend a week in boarding houses at Blackpool.

It was a poor summer on the whole, with many lives lost. The thunderstorms and gales of 27 July returned two days later; trees were felled and roofs blown away. On 5 August there were more thunderstorms, and the rivers rose. On 15 August two trains collided in Blackburn Station, injuring fifty people. On 26 August there were further fatalities after violent electrical storms.

In early September the children went back to school; a new intake of infants cowered under the mossy wall, and sought refuge in its shade from Mother Perpetua's crow-like arm.

It was after nine o'clock on a particularly wet evening late in that month that Miss Dempsey heard a knock at the front door of the presbytery. She took this ill, because it was usual for the parishioners, if in need of a priest, to come to the kitchen door at the side; the nuns, similarly, knew their place. She had not yet fed Father Angwin his evening meal, for it was the night of the Children of Mary's meeting, and Father had been obliged to give them an improving address.

The meeting had gone much as always. There had been

prayers, and Father Angwin's discourse, more rambling than usual, she thought; then a hymn to St Agnes, Protectress of the Society. There were several such hymns, all of them absurdly flattering to the saint; and Miss Dempsey, on account of her Christian name, was forced to endure both pointed disregard and scornful stares while the verses lurched on. The other Children could not bear to hear her so lauded.

> We'll sing a hymn to Agnes,
> The Martyr-Child of Rome;
> The Virgin Spouse of Jesus,
> More pure than ocean foam.

Miss Dempsey tried, during the weekly meetings – indeed she hoped she always did try – to look humble and inconspicuous; not to flaunt her status in the parish. But she felt, from the gimlet glances she received, that she was failing.

> Oh aid us, holy Agnes,
> A joyous song to raise;
> To trumpet forth thy glory,
> To sound afar thy praise.

Father Angwin said that he liked this particular hymn, did he not? He said he liked the thought of the Children of Mary blowing trumpets. But a small sigh escaped him, just the same.

After the concluding prayers the other Children were at liberty to go to the school hall to conduct the social part of their business: strong tea, parlour games and character assassination. She herself, knowing her duty, had taken off her cloak at the back of the church, handed it to the president of the Sodality, taken off her ribbon and her medal and hurried through the sacristy and back into her kitchen. She was aware that this proceeding gave the Children every opportunity to shred her reputation, but that could not be helped; on a bad night like this, Father was not to be left with a sandwich.

So who can this possibly be at the door, she wondered. She took off her pinny and hung it up. Perhaps someone is near death, and their sorrowing relatives are here to ask Father to come and give Extreme Unction. Perhaps, even, one of the Children of Mary has met with an accident; a fatal scalding with the tea urn was always a possibility. Or perhaps, she thought, it is some poor sinner, with blood on his hands, ridden over the wild moors to ask for absolution. But glancing up at the clock she knew this could not be so, for the last bus from Glossop had passed through twenty minutes earlier.

Miss Dempsey opened the door a crack. There was a bluish wild darkness outside, and rain rattled past her into the hall. Before her was a tall, dim shape, a man wrapped in a dark cloak, holes for mouth and eyes, a hat pulled over the brow; then, as her eyes became accustomed to the exterior murk, she distinguished the figure of a young man, holding in his left hand what appeared to be a doctor's black bag.

'Flood,' said the apparition.

'Indeed it is. A flood and a half.'

'No,' he said. 'F-L-U-D-D.'

A gust of wind ripped at the trees behind him; their branches, fitfully lit by the storm flickering over Nether-houghton, stretched across his tilted cheek, in a tracery like fingers or lace. 'Is this the time for a spelling bee?' Miss Dempsey flung back the door. 'Do you really consider it is?'

The young man stepped inside. Rivulets of water cascaded from his clothes and pooled on the floor of the hall. He fixed her with his gaze, and peeled off his outer layers to reveal a black suit and clerical collar. 'My name,' he said. 'F-L-U-D-D. My name is Fludd.'

So you are the curate, she thought. She felt a sudden urge to say, M-U-D-D; mine, Father, is Mudd. Then his eyes fastened upon her face.

The urge reached her lips, and died. The night chill crept into her, from the open door, and, as she went to close it, she began to tremble, and she clamped her jaws, to stop her teeth from chattering audibly; too much shivering was a vulgar thing, she felt, and would give a bad impression. 'Excuse me,' she said. 'I'll draw the bolts. It's time. Quite late. You'll not be wanting to go out again tonight.'

She did it. She felt the young man's eyes on her back when she turned the key in the lock. 'No,' he said, 'I won't want to go out again. I've come to stay.' Deep within her, behind her cardigan and her blouse and her petticoat trimmed with scratchy nylon lace, behind her interlock vest and freckled skin, Miss Dempsey sensed a slow movement, a tiny spiral shift of matter, as if, at the very moment the curate spoke, a change had occurred: a change so minute as to baffle description, but rippling out, in its effect, to infinity. In later years, when she talked about it she would always say, *Did you ever see a pile of pennies pushed over? Did you ever see a house of cards fall down?* And whomever she spoke to would look at her, comprehension strained; she could not find the words for that sliding, slipping, tripping sensation that she felt through her entire body. Miss Dempsey felt her mortality; but, in the same instant, she felt her immortality too.

At that instant, also, Father Angwin put his head around the sitting-room door. There could be no mistake about the newcomer, for he had already assumed a proprietorial air, taking off his sodden hat and setting it down on the hall-stand, and extracting himself from his cloak. A look of alarm and distaste crossed Father Angwin's face: then stronger emotions. As Miss Dempsey was to tell a parishioner, next day: 'I really thought for a moment he might fly out against him.' She saw the priest stand poised on the threshold of the room, his frail person quivering, a dangerous golden light in his eyes. A tune began to run through her head: not of a hymn. Despite herself, she began to hum, and a moment later was appalled to hear herself break into song: *John Peel's view hulloo would awaken the dead/ Or the fox from his lair in the morning.*

'This is Miss Dempsey, my housekeeper,' Father Angwin said. 'She is deranged.'

Before she could make any apology, she saw Father Fludd reach into the inside pocket of his black suit. She waited, her fingers nervously pressed to her lips, for the newcomer to produce some papers, a scroll perhaps, embossed with the Papal seal: some document excommunicating Father Angwin for drunkenness and peculiar behaviour, and installing this young man in his stead. But the curate's hand emerged with a small flat tin. He held it out to Father Angwin, and inquired, 'Have a cheroot?'

For the rest of that evening Miss Dempsey went up and down stairs, providing as best she could for the curate's comfort. He said he would take a bath, which was not at all a usual thing on a week-night. The bathroom, one of the few in Fetherhoughton at that time, was as cold as a morgue, and the hot water a rusty unreliable trickle. Miss Dempsey penetrated the frigid upper storey of the house, a threadbare towel over her arm; and then walked again with bedlinen, Irish linen sheets that were thin and starched and icy to her touch.

She looked out a hot-water bottle, and went into the curate's room to draw the curtains, and to pass a duster over the small bedside stand, and to turn the mattress. There are those, it is said, who have entertained angels unawares; but Miss Dempsey would have liked notice. Every week she cleaned this room, but naturally the bed was not aired. There was no homely touch that she could provide, unless she had brought up a bucket of coal and laid a fire; but she could never remember seeing a fire in a bedroom, and it was better not to encourage any notions that the curate might have. She had somehow formed the idea, just by those first few moments of conversation, and by his elaborate unconcern about her singing, that besides being a priest he was a gentleman. It was an impression only, given by his manners and not his appearance, for the light in the hall was too dim for her to get much idea of what he looked like.

The walls of the upper storey, like the walls of the kitchen and the downstairs hall, were painted a deep institutional green; the panelled doors were varnished with a yellowish stain. There was no lampshade in the curate's room, just a clear bulb, and the hard-edged shadows it cast. The floorboards creaked in the corridor, and Miss Dempsey stopped, rocking a little on her feet, detecting the point of the greatest noise. Downstairs the floors were made of stone. In every room a crucifix hung, the dying God in each case exhibiting some distinction of anguish, some greater or lesser contortion of his naked body, a musculature more or less racked. The house was a prison for these dying Christs, a mausoleum.

But when Miss Dempsey thought of the bishop's house, she imagined table-lamps with silk shades, and dining tables on pedestals, and an effulgence of hot electric air. When she thought of the sycophants she imagined them lolling on cushions, eating Brazil nuts. She imagined that they got food in sauces, and port wine on quite ordinary days, and rinsed their fingers in holy water in little marble basins; that in the grounds of the bishop's house, where the sycophants walked together plotting in Latin, there were fountains and statuary and a dovecote. Crossing the hall, she paused outside the sitting-room door. She heard conversation in full spate. She could tell that Father Angwin had been drinking whisky. The curate spoke in his light, dry voice: 'In considering the life of Christ, there is something that has often made me wonder; did the man who owned the Gadarene swine get compensation?'

Miss Dempsey tiptoed away.

The curate moved his hand over the tablecloth, in a skimming motion, sweeping the topic aside. His fingers – bloodless, pointed fingers – floated over the linen like swans on a lake of milk.

'I thought you might be one of those modern fellows,' Father Angwin said. 'I thought you might have no scholarship. I was sick to think about it.'

Father Fludd looked down, with an inward modest smile, as if disclaiming any pretensions. He had been drinking too, but he was certainly not drunk; despite the hour – and it was now eleven o'clock – he was as pleasant, mild and breezy as if it were teatime. Whenever Father Angwin looked up at him, it seemed that his whisky glass was raised to his lips, but the level of what was in it did not seem to go down; and yet from time to time the young man reached out for the bottle, and topped himself up. It had been the same with their late dinner; there were three sausages (from the Co-op butcher) on Father Fludd's plate, and he was always cutting into one or other, and spearing a bit on his fork; he was always chewing in an unobtrusive, polite way, with his mouth shut tight. And yet there were always three sausages on his plate, until at last, quite suddenly, there were none. Father Angwin's first thought was that Fludd had a small dog concealed about his person, in the way that starlets conceal their pooches from the customs men; he had seen this in the newspaper. But Fludd, unlike the starlets, had not got his neck sunk into a fur; and then again, Father Angwin thought, would a dog drink so much whisky?

From time to time, also, the curate leant forward and busied himself building up the fire. He was a handy type with the tongs, Father Angwin could tell. His efforts were keeping the room remarkably warm; and yet when Agnes came in, lugging a bucket of coal, she checked herself in surprise and said, 'You don't need this.'

Presently Father Angwin got up, and opened the window a crack. 'It makes a change, for this house,' he said, 'but it's as hot as hell.'

'Though far better ventilated,' said Fludd, sipping his whisky.

It's time they had cocoa, Miss Dempsey thought. They'll be tumbling under the table. The bishop will have chosen this toper, to lead poor Angwin on; he had a good head for drink, that was for sure, and no doubt when Angwin had passed out he would be tiptoeing into the hall and lifting the receiver on his special telephone line to His Corpulence.

And yet Miss Dempsey was not sure what to think. That look he had given her, in the hall; was it not, for all its chilling nature, a look of deep compassion? Could it be that Fludd was not a sycophant, but some innocent that the bishop wished to ruin? She felt that look still: as if her flesh had become glass.

I'll sing again, she thought, to impress on him that if I'm given to singing it's usually something pious. I'll just hum as I take in this tray. She spread on the tray a white cloth with a scalloped edge, embroidered with satin-stitch pansies, which she had purchased in June at the parish Sale of Work; it looked, she thought, more pure than ocean foam. She placed the cups of cocoa upon it, and then two plates, and on each plate three Rich Tea biscuits. *To Christ thy heart was given,/ The world pursued in vain . . .*

She knocked; no reply of course, they were talking again. *Its promises ne'er moved thee . . .* She shoved open the door with her foot, and manoeuvred herself in. The heat took her aback; the fire was roaring up the chimney. She lost the thread of her verse. The curate looked up at her and smiled as she put the tray on the table, and she looked back, full into his face; this time, she thought, I must be sure and form some notion of what he looks like. She held his gaze for what length of time she could, without appearing to stare; and then bent over the hearth, touching the tiles up quite needlessly with the little gilt brush from the fireside set. She surprised herself; she usually brought in a filthy, bristly kitchen-type of brush for this job, and at the thought of anyone violating the fireside set she would have spat.

She waited for Father Angwin to say, as he usually did, these are boring biscuits, I like Fig, I like Custard Creams; but he was entirely caught up in his conversation with the curate, his hands knotting and unknotting on the table, a flurry of agitation in his voice. 'I try to tell myself that whatever evil is done is done *permettio dei*, with God's sanction –'

'I understand,' said the curate gravely.

'– and certainly Augustine argues most persuasively in *The City of God* that though good can exist without evil, evil cannot exist without good. And yet the feeling has taken hold of me that the devil has got his independence in this world. It is he who has got the reins in his hands, I feel.'

Father Fludd stirred his cocoa, judiciously. His eyes were downcast.

'I'll come in for the tray,' Agnes said. 'I like to get washed up before bedtime, Father. If there's one thing I cannot abide it's to see dirty pots first thing in the morning. I think it's a habit low in the extreme.'

'I don't know *where* God is,' Father Angwin said. 'I don't know *that* he is.'

'Drink it while it's hot,' Agnes said to him, 'and don't get yourself worked up before bedtime.'

But Father Angwin was not listening to her. He looked through her as if he were not seeing her, and for a moment she felt an uprush of fear, like cold water on the back of her neck; what if she were really not visible, what if Father Fludd had disappeared her in some way? The next moment, her good sense reasserted itself. She went out into the hall, humming: *All vain the wooer's pleading/ All vain the judge's ire:/ One love alone thy bosom/ Inflamed with chastest fire.* Was not 'bosom' a rude word? But you were always getting it in hymns. Miss Dempsey had no terms at all for some sections of her anatomy; she never paid them attention. *As men go to a banquet* . . . She tried to remember what Father Fludd looked like, but the pattern of his features had been cleanly erased from her mind.

'So one morning,' Father Angwin went on, 'I woke up. This was twenty years ago. It had gone in the night.'

'I see,' said Father Fludd.

'How can you explain that? I had it at night, and in the morning it had gone. I felt for the first quarter of an hour that it might come to light, in the way, you know, you might kick your slippers under the bed, or be absent-minded with your toothbrush.'

Father Fludd leant forward; they had transferred themselves now to the two armchairs, and sat at either side of the fire. 'Did you apply to St Anthony? You know he is the nonpareil for finding what is lost.'

'But how could I?' Father Angwin threw out his hands, in a large and liberal gesture of despair. 'How could I, considering the nature of my loss, apply to Anthony or any other saint?'

'I suppose not,' Fludd said. 'There are some losses – virginity, for instance – that St Anthony could do nothing about – but you would not be debarred from asking him, if you were an optimist. Your situation, it seems to me, was more grave than the loss of virginity. What did you do next?'

'I looked in the wardrobe, I think. I got up – it was five o'clock, still dark – and I went and looked in the sacristy. I opened the press up and felt among the vestments. I knew there was no chance, but you can imagine how it was. I was half out of my mind with fear of the future.'

'And then?'

'I looked on the altar. It wasn't there. It had vanished while I slept, and I had to accept the fact.' Father Angwin's head drooped. 'I had lost my faith. I no longer believed in God at all.'

'You relive the moment,' Fludd said, 'as if it were yesterday. May I ask what you did next?'

Father Angwin placed his hands together, fingertip to fingertip. He considered. 'It seemed to me, that what I had urgent need of was some kind of survival plan, some kind of strategy. I wondered, is there a diocesan House of Detention for priests in my case? Somewhere they are put to be kept from view? After all, you cannot stop being a priest, can you? No matter how faithless or scandalous a man is, once he is a priest he is a priest for all eternity. I couldn't abscond, could I, I couldn't do a moonlight flit?'

'I should say your way was plain,' Fludd said. 'A man may preserve the outward form, if he lacks the inward grace.'

'Yes. So I thought, well, I have no faith, I must just pretend I have.'

'And may I venture a guess? You had a parish. It must be served. And yet you would feel – what? On shaky ground. Suppose you made a slip, gave yourself away?'

'I was a charlatan,' Father Angwin said. 'A pretender. A fake. Do you know what worried me? That I would stop thinking like a priest. Stop talking like a priest. That one day some parishioner would come at me with some question – is this or that a sin, should I do that or the other – and I'd say, well, what do *you* think, what do you feel like doing, what does your common sense tell you?'

'Common sense has nothing to do with religion,' Father Fludd said reprovingly. 'And personal opinion has little to do with sin.'

'Exactly. Just my point. I was afraid I'd forget myself, respond as any person might – appeal, as it were, to the human and not the divine. I had to safeguard myself. Against this grievous peril.'

'So did you then become scrupulous? Did you become

exacting?' Fludd leant forward in his chair, his eyes alight. 'Did you make a point of it to become known in the district for the strictness of your opinions, for your old-fashioned stances, for the rigidity of your views? You would not hear of any innovation, deviation: of any slight departure from the rules of Lenten fasting, say? You would not remit a jot or a tittle?'

'That is about the size of it.' Father Angwin looked morose; he slumped a little. 'Any more in that bottle?'

Fludd had secreted it by his chair, it seemed. He reached down, and poured his senior a generous measure. 'Wonderful,' Father Angwin murmured. 'Go on now, Father Fludd. You seem to be on my trail.'

'Shall we say, for instance, that in the confessional you gave no leeway? Supposing, for instance, some woman with six children came along. What did you recommend?'

'Oh, you know, I said they must abstain.'

'What did they say to that?'

'They said, thank you, Father.'

'They were relieved?'

'The word does not convey the measure of their jubilation. The men of Fetherhoughton are not noted for romance.'

'And if they said to you, Father, I cannot abstain, for the brute insists on his pleasures?'

'I said, then there is no help for it, my dear, you must have six more.'

'I understand,' Fludd said. 'Suppose as a good Catholic you meet some very particular hardship, some tiny absurdity, which, as you imagine, is making life very hard for some poor son or daughter of the Church. You think, well now, what can this matter? What can it signify, in the eternal scheme of things? I will just, in this little instance, separate my judgement from the traditions of the Church. But faith, Father Angwin, is like a wall, a big, blank, brick wall. One day, some fool comes with a hairpin, and chooses some inch of it, and begins to scrape away at the mortar. When the first dust flies up, the wall falls down.'

Father Angwin took a draught of his whisky. What Fludd said was comprehensible entirely; and he imagined the bishop, producing some dusty, purloined hairpin from the hot depth of his pocket. 'I thought to myself,' he said, 'a priest must believe in God, or at least pretend to; and who knows, if I pretend for thirty years, for forty years, perhaps the belief will grow back in again, the mask will grow into the flesh. And if you can accept the preposterous notion of a living creator who gives a bugger about every sparrow that falls, why jib at the rest of it? Why jib at rosaries and relics and fasting and abstinence? Why swallow a camel and strain at a gnat? And with that as my philosophy, it somehow seemed possible to go on, enclosed in ritual, safe as houses, as they say. Oh, the central premise was missing, but do you know, it didn't seem to matter all that much? You wouldn't think it, would you? You'd think if you lost your faith you couldn't continue in this life. But I can assure you – this is the one life you can continue in.'

'You made an accommodation,' Fludd said. 'It is natural. Suppose a woman marries a man, after some great love affair. Then one morning she wakes up beside the chap, and sees that he is a mere nothing, despicable, a blot on her landscape. Does she rise up from her bed and go about the streets proclaiming her error? No, she does not. She gets back under the bedclothes. For the rest of the day she is even more civil to him than she has been before.'

'I dare say you are right,' Father Angwin said. 'I dare say the parallel can be drawn. But I have not given much thought to the married state. I put it to myself differently. I thought, suppose your heart were taken out? But you could still walk and talk, and have your breakfast. Well, you wouldn't miss it, would you?'

'So,' said Father Fludd, 'you walked about the district

without your heart, and you continued to hear confessions and say early Mass, you did all that was required of you and more; you travelled your necessary way, fettered as you were to this stale bridegroom, the Church. You didn't shout from the pulpit that you no longer believed in God.'

'Why should I? If the heathen in his blindness bows down to wood and stone, why should not the Fetherhoughtonians do the same? Oh, I'd be willing, as the bishop says I ought, to deliver them from their ignorance: but what would I deliver them to?'

'It is a question,' Fludd said. 'But now, what is this problem you have with the devil? How can it be that your belief in him remains?'

'Well, I saw him,' Father Angwin said, rather curtly. 'He hangs about the parish.' He was silent for a moment, recovering his manners. 'My dear boy, could I prevail upon you to drink that cocoa? I see you have stirred it up, and then taken no further interest in it. I wouldn't wish you to provoke Agnes, on your first night. She believes cocoa is good for priests.'

Fludd picked up his cup. 'What did he look like?'

'The devil? He was a little man in a checked cap. He had one of those round faces, apple-cheeked, you'd say.'

'And you had never seen him before?'

'Oh, I'd seen him many a time. He comes from Nether-houghton. He keeps a shop. A tobacconist, he is. But don't you understand, Father, how you can look and look at a thing, perhaps all the days of your life, without knowing its true nature at all? Until one day light dawns?'

'I would not say in this instance that it was light. I would say it was darkness.'

'That afternoon,' Father Angwin picked up his own cup, and inspected its contents, 'that afternoon, I say, I was walking about the church grounds, making my circuit around the convent and the school, just having a think to myself.

And there the fellow appeared to me, just bobbed up from nowhere, and raised his cap. He smiled at me – and by God, I knew him.'

'How did you know him?'

'It was his smile . . . his horrible jauntiness . . . the little tune he whistled.'

'Anything else?

'Perhaps the smell of sulphur. It stank out the afternoon.'

'Sulphur,' said Fludd, 'may be taken as definitive.'

Agnes put her head around the door. She cleared her throat. 'Are you finished with the tray?' The rest of her appeared. 'It's bedtime,' she said. 'We keep decent hours, Father Fludd.'

'Agnes,' Father Angwin said, 'Father Fludd is not obliged to go to bed just because you are going.'

'It's not a matter of obligation,' Agnes said. 'It's a matter of seemliness. I've already locked up, hours ago.'

'Good,' Father Angwin said. 'If there is anything we want, we shall get it ourselves. Father Fludd, I daresay, knows how to boil a kettle.'

Miss Dempsey went out, and double-checked the big bolts on the front door, rattling them as she did so; not in protest at being sent about her business, but as a counter to the deep calm that had fallen on the house. The storm was over. When she looked through the kitchen window, she could see that the trees still swayed, but only a little, like polite dancers on a crowded floor. And any noise they made was lost to her, shut out by thick stone walls and the evening's events. She touched her lip, fingering the small flat protuberance there. She turned off the light and went up to bed, leaving the dirty cocoa cups in the sink; departing from the habit of a lifetime, feeling that her life was somehow altered. It was true that the curate had not spoken to her, apart from an exchange of pleasantries, a few words when she brought in the sausages. But there was a whisper at the back of her mind, and only he could have put it there: I have come to transform you, transformation is my business.

The two men sat on, talking through the night. Soon it came, the peevish dawn. The fire fell to ash. Father Angwin felt his way upstairs in the dark, his hand against the wall. He had an hour or two before he must be up to say Mass. He lay down, removing only his shoes, and fell at once into a deep sleep.

When he woke up, he did not know what time it was. His mouth felt dry, there was unaccustomed sun outside the window. He lay thinking, not caring about anything very much. It seemed possible – probable, even – that he had dreamt Father Fludd. The details of their conversation were remarkably clear, but he found that he could not call the young man's face to mind. Bits of it he could get: an eye, the nose. He could not somehow fit it together. It seemed possible that Fludd was some composite figure he had got out of his imagination; perhaps he had fallen asleep before the fire.

He sat up, rubbed his palms over his face, put the heel of his hands into his eyes and rubbed them, stroked his chin and thought of shaving, conversed mentally with his empty stomach and promised it a digestible coddled egg. Then, in his stockinged feet, his shoes in his hand, he crept down the passage and pushed open the door of the curate's room.

It was not empty. Fludd was in bed and asleep. He lay on his back, staring sightlessly at the ceiling, and his reserved, almost severe expression forbade Father Angwin's close inspection. The room smelled of incense. Father Fludd wore some kind of old-fashioned nightshirt, starched and with a ruffled collar; it was a pattern that Father Angwin had never seen before, and immediately it excited his envy.

He turned away and tiptoed from the room, closing the door softly behind him; though it did not seem to him, as he remarked later, that an earthquake would have disturbed the curate. He looked like a bishop upon his catafalque; immediately this image occurred to him, Father Angwin thought bishop, bishop, we had no discussion of the bishop last night. His name was not even mentioned. If Fludd is a spy, I am ruined; but would any spy sleep so soundly? Then he thought, I am ruined anyway.

And there was the housekeeper, downstairs, about her morning round, and singing once more – Miss Dempsey, he thought, had conceit of her voice – to impress that oblivious, motionless, waxen image in the room behind him. He wondered, for an instant, whether he should return and take the curate's pulse. But no: if Father Fludd was in the habit of dying during the night, that was a matter for himself. A fragment came back to him from last night's conversation; had not the curate quoted Voltaire? 'It is no more surprising to be born twice than to be born once.'

Father Angwin put out a hand, to steady himself. He was overwhelmed with hunger; he felt quite giddy and faint. I must persuade Agnes, he thought, to forgive me my trespasses, and let me have two eggs. She was in the kitchen now, pursuing in her uncertain soprano the theme of the martyrdom of St Agnes:

> As men go to a banquet,
> As bride to meet her groom;
> So thou with joyous footsteps
> Didst haste to meet thy doom.
> The soldiers wept in pity,
> The headsman blushed for shame;
> One sign alone escaped thee.
> 'Twas Jesus' sweetest name.

Chapter Four

That afternoon, Father Fludd undertook a parish tour. Father
Angwin conducted the curate to the front door. 'They may
ask you into their houses,' he said. 'For God's sake don't eat
anything. Be back before dark.' He hovered, anxious. 'Perhaps you shouldn't go alone?'

'Don't fuss, man,' Fludd said.

Father Angwin felt the weight of his responsibility. He had
taken to the boy; the topic of the bishop lay uneasily between
them, but since so far there had been no communication
from that quarter, Father Angwin assumed that Fludd was
not much in favour. He imagined that the bishop would be
disconcerted by Fludd; that he would feel threatened by his
scholarship, and affronted by his way of getting to the heart
of a matter. No doubt, then, the parish was to become a
dumping ground; Fludd was a discard, like himself.

'Here,' he said, 'take this umbrella. The glass has been
falling. There was a halo around the moon. It will rain
before evening.'

Fludd accepted the umbrella; the two priests shook hands
formally, and then Fludd strode out downhill.

On the carriage-drive, he met a bunch of little wild-looking
children. They had scabs on their knees, and their heads
were shaved to deter lice. Each one of them clung on to the
neck of his misshapen jersey.

'We saw an ambulance, Father,' they said. '*Touch my shoulder, touch my knee, Pray to God it won't be me.* Then we have to hang on to us collars till we see a white dog.'

'But you haven't got collars,' Fludd said.

'Where they would be, if we had,' the children explained; and one small girl said, 'We have to make do.'

'I see,' Fludd said. 'Well, I hope you see a white dog soon. Do they do this all over the district?'

'Not in Netherhoughton,' the children said, after some thought; the girl added, 'The ambulances don't go up there.'

Fludd was curious. 'Who told you that you must do this?'

The children looked at each other. They could not remember being told. It was a thing that they had always known. A few of them said, 'Mother Purpit.' The little girl said, 'God.'

Father Fludd passed the school gates, and soon the rough track ceased to be the carriage-drive and became Church Street; there were cobbles underfoot, and high hedges, grey in aspect, leaves drooping. Through their gaps he glimpsed fields, hummocks of coarse grass flattening in the wind. He stopped to examine a leaf; he wetted his finger, and passed it over the surface, which felt greasy, with an overlay of fine grit. He licked his finger; it tasted of soil and smoke. Below him he saw the mill chimneys of Fetherhoughton, like pillars for stylites, or the towers on which heathens place their dead.

In Upstreet, matrons with baskets over their arms stood in knots, and interrupted their talk to stare at him as he went by. He raised a hand; half-greeting, half-blessing. He turned off into Chapel Street, the ground climbing steeply again; he pictured himself knocking at each of these doors, making himself known. At number 30, a woman was kneeling in the open doorway, whitening her step with donkey stone. He stood and watched her, uncertain whether to speak; then, thinking himself without manners, strode on. A little way ahead of him other doors opened; housewives appeared, and with a big heave of their elbows hauled on to the pavement buckets of soapy water. Head first, crouching, they intruded into his view like dogs coming out of their kennels, and set to work with their scrubbing brushes. Their flowered pinnies were secured tightly, taped round their middles and round again. Each placed to hand her donkey stone: some palest cream, some mushroom colour, some a deep butterscotch, others as yellow as best butter. Their elbows jutted as they scrubbed, their jerseys rolled up beyond the joint; he saw their fine, bluish skin, the labouring swell of their slack abdomens, the tops of their heads with the fading hair.

He pitied these women. Several of them, Father Angwin said, had lost their husbands in the Council House Riots of the previous year. The site of the riots – razed now – seemed to smoke still in the afternoon air; and where the men had fallen, each asserting his right to the fat of the land, impromptu crosses were stuck in the rubbly ground. 'Either they should have built houses for all of them,' Father Angwin said, 'or none at all.' Last night he had spoken of those days as his worst in Fetherhoughton: the gangs of muttering, mutinous women, handbags filled with kitchen knives and bottles of paraffin; the misspelt placards on the church door; and finally, one summer afternoon, the call to say that the constabulary had moved in, that there were casualties, that the fire brigade was on its way.

Opposite the site of the riots stood the Methodist chapel, a low-browed, red-brick building; it was from within its door that the first wave of rioters had burst, with their anti-Papist battle-cries. Father Fludd accorded it a searching glance, then set out across the Methodist graveyard, where some of the Protestant fatalities had been laid to rest. He vaulted the low wall, and found himself on Back Lane; he turned right, up the hill towards Netherhoughton.

Back Lane was hardly alive to his presence; a couple of

women came out and leant in their doorways, watching him with impassive faces, and one of them called out that he might come in and she would brew tea. Remembering Father Angwin's warning, he raised his hat to her, courteously, and showed by a gesture that he must hurry on. 'Turn back,' the woman said, and laughed scornfully; then went in, slamming her door.

Soon the houses ran out; the street narrowed, became a lane. There was a good three-mile tramp, Father Angwin had told him, around the loop of unfrequented road that would take him towards the hamlet and the moors. And no shelter, not a house or a tree, simply the moors on the traveller's right hand, and on the left unfenced fields that had once been allotments. It was the railway workers who had rented them, for here you were not far, as the crow flies, from Fetherhoughton's small branch-line station. Besides growing vegetables, some of them had kept hens, even an occasional pig. But the coops and sties were empty now and damply rotting. The raiding parties had come down from Netherhoughton, and carried off the spring greens, and at last the men had grown weary of patching and mending their fences, and replanting what was torn out. They had abandoned the site, and told their wives to frequent the Co-op greengrocers; the fields were reverting rapidly to their waste-ground character, and the only sign that the railway men had once been there was a red spotted kerchief, tied to a crumbling fence pole, and whipping defiantly in the breeze.

Father Fludd halted, and looked at the empty road before him; he felt chilled and tired. He fished in his pocket for the sketch map that Father Angwin had drawn for him, and saw that if he were to retrace his steps, down Back Lane to Upstreet, a short climb would bring him to the station yard, and from there a footpath cut straight across the fields to Netherhoughton's main street. He squashed the map back into his pocket, and turned on his heel; as he passed the house where the woman had offered him tea, he thought he saw a curtain shift at an upper window.

Upstreet was largely deserted now. Once you had done your shopping, he supposed, there was nothing to detain you. He looked at his watch; it was almost five o'clock, and the inhospitable chill of an autumn evening was already in the air, a compound miasma of leaf-mould, coal fires, wet wool, cough syrup.

As he neared the station, Fludd saw advancing upon him another gang of juveniles, older this time, more orderly, a dozen or so adolescents in tight formation. These young Fetherhoughtonians were the pupils of the grammar school in the nearest town. They were few but conspicuous; their maroon school uniforms, bought large so that they could grow into them, stood out from their bodies like the dark capes of Crusaders. There was a wary, darting-eyed expression on the faces of the gawky lads of eighteen, their little caps on their heads, satchels like postage stamps slung over their great bony shoulders. Some of the girls carried cake tins, held against their bodies like shields, and others had bags of knitting, from which metal needles poked; the boys carried wood-working tools which they did not trouble to hide. The outriders of the group, grim-faced girls of twelve and thirteen, bore their hockey sticks at a vigilant, offensive angle.

'Good evening,' the priest said. 'I am the new curate, Fludd's my name. How are you enjoying the new term?'

Startled, offended eyes passed over him. As he stood in their path they could not proceed, and, unwilling to break ranks, they came to a halt.

'May we pass?' said one of the stick-wielding girls.

'I was only wondering,' Fludd said, 'what the young such as yourselves find to do in this place.'

'Our homework,' said a voice from the centre of the group.

'Do you not find yourselves with a bit of free time at the weekend?'

'We don't go out,' the girl said firmly. 'We don't want fights with teddy boys.'

'We stay in,' another voice said; adding, in explanation, 'It is called bettering ourselves. We have to get into Manchester University.'

'Do you come to Mass?' Fludd said. 'We could have a meeting after. We could have games. Table-tennis.'

The children looked at each other. Their expressions softened; one of the small boys said, with a lingering regret, 'We are atheists.'

'I don't think that would be a good idea at all,' the girl said. 'You see, Father, our parents won't let us outside without we put our uniforms on, and it attracts trouble.'

The little boy said, 'Them from Thomas Aquinas bash us up.'

'They'll be upon us now,' the girl said, 'if you don't excuse us.'

Behind her, in unison, three girls held out their cake tins, and rattled them in unison: *odi, odas, odat.*

'I hate,' the girl explained balefully. 'You hate. He she or it hates.'

'You need not go on,' Fludd murmured. 'I know the rest.'

'Nothing personal,' a large boy said; and the rattlers, holding their cake tins aloft, explained, 'We pelt 'em with our domestic science.'

Fludd stood aside and watched them go, their heads swivelling to check the doorways of the shops. In the station yard he climbed over the stile that let him on to the footpath, and struck out across country, swiping at the tussocks of grass with Father Angwin's umbrella. The incline, slight at first, became steeper, and he stopped to catch his breath before mounting the next stile; he handed himself over it, and found himself in Netherhoughton's main street.

It proved to be a straggling settlement, with two dilapi-
dated inns, the Old Oak and the Ram; a tobacconist's shop,
shuttered, which must surely be the one Father Angwin had
mentioned: a general grocer, with a pyramid of tea packets
in the window: and a baker, whose shelves were quite empty
except for the sleeping form of a large black cat. The cottages
here were of a different design, some of them only one room
deep; low, sway-backed roofs showed their age, and he
noted at once the Netherhoughtonian habit of bricking up
any window deemed superfluous. All about him he saw the
lively signs of alchemy: the black hens scratching in the small
back-plots, and the nine-runged ladder, the *scala philoso-
phorum*, leaning casually against a wall. He walked on until
the houses petered out, and he reached the rusting iron gate
that gave on to the moorland paths. He stood for a moment,
looking up into the wild landscape and the rushing sky, and
as he turned away he felt the first drops of rain on his face.

He put up the providential umbrella, and retraced his
steps down the lane. Before he had time to turn up the collar
of his cape a thick and viscid-seeming mist had crept up
around him. In the failing light the dirty windowpanes
seemed opaque, as if thinly curtained with lead. Shivering, he
huddled against a wall, and studied his map again; another
footpath, branching off the one that had brought him there,
would take him across the former allotments and bring him
out within ten minutes, he calculated, at the back of the
convent.

He must pay his courtesy call on the nuns soon, in fact
today; otherwise they might be offended. No doubt, out of
Christian charity, they would offer him some hot chocolate:
buttered biscuits perhaps: even teacakes and jam. They would
be glad of a visitor. Climbing once more over the stile, he
smiled to himself; and with fresh heart picked up his feet out
of the thickening mud.

*

The parlour in the convent was both stuffy and cold, and smelled mysteriously of congealed gravy. It was little used; Fludd sat by the empty fireplace, on a hard chair, waiting for Mother Purpit. Under his feet was dark, shiny linoleum in a pattern of parquet squares, relieved by a red fireside rug. Over the mantelpiece, Christ hung in a heavy gilt frame, thin yellow tongues of light streaming from his head. His ribcage was open, neatly split by the Roman spear, and with a pallid, pointed finger he indicated his exposed and perfectly heart-shaped heart.

Against the far wall was a big, heavy chest with a stout-looking iron lock; oak, it might be, but varnished with a heavy hand over the years, so that its surface seemed sticky and repelled the light. I wonder what is in that chest, thought Fludd. Nuns' requisites; now what would they be?

Tired of waiting, he shifted on his chair. The chest tempted him; his eyes were drawn to it, back and back again. He got up, froze in mid-movement as the chair creaked; then took courage, and crept across the room. He tested the lid of the chest, gingerly; it didn't give. He shifted it an inch, to see how heavy it was: very.

There was a footstep behind him. He straightened up, smiling easily. Mother Perpetua cleared her throat – too late to give a friendly warning, but just in time to make a point – then crossed to the tall, narrow windows and drew the curtains. 'Nights drawing in,' she observed.

'Mm,' Fludd said.

'Our clothes,' Purpit said. She indicated the chest. 'It is our clothes that we brought with us when we left the world. I keep the key.'

'About your person?'

Purpit declined to answer. 'It is a responsibility,' she said 'overseeing the welfare of so many souls.'

'So you are both headmistress, and superior of the convent, are you?'

Purpit tossed her veil, as if to say, who else could do it? Father Fludd studied the chest. 'Could I look into it, do you think?' he asked.

'Oh, I don't think so.'

'Is there some rule to forbid it?'

'I should think there is.'

'Is it your nature to assume so?'

'I must. Suppose the bishop were to find out?' Mother Perpetua came up behind him and stooped over the chest, proprietorially. Then she cast an eye up at him, sideways, from behind the jutting edge of her headdress. It was as if a blinkered horse had winked. 'Still, Father, I suppose I might make an exception. I suppose I might be prevailed upon.'

'After all,' Fludd said, 'there cannot be any harm in looking at empty clothes. And there must be some curious modes in that box.'

Perpetua patted the lid of the chest; she had a large hand, with prominent knuckles. 'I could gratify you,' she said. 'Your curiosity. After all . . .' She eased herself to the vertical, and let her eyes wander over him. 'I suppose the bishop's not likely to hear of it. If you don't tell him, and I don't.' She slid a hand into the folds of her robes, below the waist, and fumbled there, and presently drew out a large, old-fashioned iron key.

'It must be a weight for you to carry about,' Fludd observed.

'I can assure you, Father, it is the least of my burdens.' Mother Perpetua fitted the key into the lock. 'Allow me,' Fludd said.

He wrestled with the lock. At first, no success. 'It is not often opened,' Perpetua said. 'Once a decade is as much. There are not many vocations these days.' Fludd knelt, and applied force; there was a grind, scrape, click, and it gave at last. He raised the lid of the chest with a slow reverence, as if he might find human remains within; which indeed, he thought, you might say that I do, for in this chest are the remains of all worldly vanities. Did not Ignatius himself compare those in religion to the dead, when he enjoined on them obedience, each to their very own Mother Perpetua? 'Each one,' said the saint, 'should give himself up into the hands of his superiors, just as a dead body allows itself to be treated in any way whatever.'

At once a powerful smell of mothballs rose up. 'I'm not sure why we bother to preserve them whole,' Perpetua said. 'It's not as if anyone is going anywhere in them.'

Fludd reached into the chest, and lifted up the topmost garment, letting it fall out of its folds. It was a little white muslin frock with a sailor collar, its wide skirt meant, he thought, just to clear the ankle. 'Whose would this be?'

'I dare say Sister Polycarp's. She always claimed a fondness for the Senior Service.'

The nun plunged her hand into the chest, and brought out a pair of navy-blue shoes, with two-bar straps and waisted heels. Next came a navy-blue serge suit, of similar vintage, with a fitted waist and a bell-shaped skirt. 'Who's to know which is whose? Three came in together, more or less. They're of an age. Now then – what about this hat?'

Father Fludd took it from her and stroked the felt, and pricked his fingers on the bunch of stubby, fierce-looking grey feathers.

'I can picture Sister Cyril in that. Or Sister Ignatius Loyola, either one. Oh, dear God.' Purpit gave a whoop of laughter. 'Here's their underthings all wrapped up. Here's their corsets.'

There were three pairs of corsets rolled together: one Twilfit, two Excelsior. Fludd held them up, like a map of the world, and let them unroll with a clatter. Purpit giggled. 'Oh, Father,' she said. 'This is not for your eyes, I'm sure.'

She plunged her arm into the chest, ferreting around at the bottom. 'Dear God,' she said, 'a hobble skirt. Well, that takes care of the three of them.'

Father Fludd picked out a straw boater, and turned it in his hands. It had a dark-blue ribbon.

'That must belong to Sister Anthony. She's the oldest of all. This will be her tweed suit. Her summer tweed.' Purpit held it up against herself. 'Well now, will you look at the size she was? Almost what she is now.'

He imagined Sister Anthony, a healthy creature with flushed cheeks, jumping down from a pony and trap, on the carriage-drive; the year, 1900. Mother Perpetua shook out a pair of silk combinations, with lace-trimmed legs, and buttons down the front. 'She must have fancied herself in these.'

'What happens,' Fludd asked, 'if you are sent to another convent of the Order? Do your effects follow you about? Do you pack a case?'

'Oh, we wouldn't carry them ourselves. Suppose we were run over and taken to hospital? And they opened up the case? They wouldn't believe we were nuns at all. They would think we belonged to a concert-party.'

'They are sent after you, then.'

'They come by the carrier. Though I see,' she said, sifting through what remained in the chest, 'that we don't have anything here for Philomena. Not that it's a loss, the kind of jumble-sale tat that I imagine a girl like her would have been wearing when she turned up as a postulant. But now isn't that typical Ireland for you? Send the nun, and no clothes, just forget about it –' Mother Purpit let her jaw hang vacantly, and assumed a glassy-eyed expression – 'just let the world go by. You should have seen the state of her when she presented herself here. An old Gladstone bag in her hand, tied up with string, and that nearly empty. I've heard of holy poverty, but in my opinion you can go too far. One pair of stockings, and those in holes, her clodhopper's toe poking through. When her handkerchiefs last saw starch, I wouldn't care to speculate.'

'She sounds more than anything like a displaced person,' Fludd said.

'I'd displace her back again, if I had my way, Father. But I don't, more's the pity. It's Mother Provincial who gives the marching orders.' Indignation had taken over Mother Perpetua; she forgot that he did not know what she was talking about. 'But I told her, Mother Provincial, I told her straight. I said if the girl wants to go in for that sort of thing, she should have taken herself off to some contemplatives; we Sisters of the Holy Innocents have to keep our heads screwed on, we have good solid practical work to do. I said to Mother Provincial, don't think I'm going to allow my convent to become some repository for the Order's embarrassments, because I won't have it. I'll speak to the bishop.'

'Heavens,' Fludd said. 'What had Sister Philomena done?'

'She'd made claims for herself.'

'What variety of claims?'

'She said she had the stigmata. She said her palms bled every Friday.'

'And did other people see this?'

Perpetua sniffed. '*Irish* people saw it,' she said. 'Some senile old donkey of a parish priest – forgive me, Father, but I always speak my mind – who was foolish enough to fall for her nonsense. It caused a stir, you see, had a whole parish in a state of excitement. I'm pleased to say that when he took it further the pair of them were pretty soon stamped on. At diocesan level, you know. In my experience you can count on a bishop.'

'So they sent her to England?'

'Yes, to get her out of that over-excited, unhealthy atmosphere. Well, I put it to you, Father, have you ever heard anything like it? Stigmata, indeed, in this day and age? Did you ever hear of anything in such poor taste?'

'Was she seen by a doctor?'

'Oh yes, but an *Irish* doctor could make nothing of it. I tell you, her feet had scarcely touched the ground before I arranged a good sensible man to take a proper look at her.'

She sniffed again. 'Do you know what he said it was? He said it was dermatitis.'

'And how is she now?'

'Oh, she's over it now. I've seen to that.' She broke off. 'But why are we wasting time over this fool of a girl? You'll want your tea.'

Perpetua rustled out. What a noise her habit seemed to make, crackling and rasping; how her heels thumped on the linoleum. The air around her was loud with contention; he could think of nothing less conducive to a life of prayer.

Fludd resumed his seat by the fire. Presently, he heard the nun returning – he could hear her right along the corridor, now that he was alert for her. Behind her toddled an elderly sister, rotund and beaming, bearing a tea-tray. 'Sister Anthony,' Purpit said.

'How do you do, Sister Anthony?'

'Well, in Jesus Christ, and I'm pleased to make your acquaintance, Father; won't you with your youth and all be a great help to poor auld Angwin?'

'Sister, don't be quaint,' Purpit said. 'Not in my hearing.'

Anthony sighed, and put down the tea-tray on the gate-legged table. 'You could have had a sandwich,' she said. 'You could have had fish-paste. But they said it was bad. Said it was off. Polycarp said it might have been in the desert for forty days and forty nights. I don't know. I couldn't taste anything off with it. I ate mine.'

'Sister has an excellent digestion,' said Mother Perpetua.

'Young things,' Sister Anthony said. 'Nuns today. Want coddling. Finicky.'

'Do you want coddling, Father Fludd?' Purpit asked: gaily, without malice.

He glanced at her. Her gaiety was a terrible thing to see. 'Not to worry, Sister Anthony,' he said. 'Miss Dempsey will have something for me when I get in. The tea alone will be most welcome.'

69

'And try one of the biscuits. I baked them myself just this last fortnight.'

Sister Anthony went out, moving airily despite her bulk. As Mother Perpetua busied herself with the teapot, Fludd became conscious of a noise outside the door, a low rustle, a type of dull snuffling.

'Who is there?' he inquired.

'Oh, it is Sister Polycarp, Sister Cyril and Sister Ignatius Loyola. They want to be introduced to you.'

Fludd half-rose. 'Should we not let them in?'

Perpetua smiled, and poured the milk in a thin high stream. 'In good time,' she said. She handed him his cup, with what was almost a simper: 'Is that how you like it, Father?'

Father Fludd looked down. 'I hardly know. I just drink it as it comes.'

'Ah, I might have known. You young priests. So ascetic. So unworldly.' Perpetua sighed, and supplied herself generously with sugar. 'I suppose the bishop is very proud of you.'

Fludd tested his tea, hedgingly. 'Do you think so?'

'Else why would he send you here to sort out this mess, if he didn't put his absolute faith in you? Oh, you're young, of course, to take on a wily old fox like Father Angwin – and by the way, he drinks, you know, and he has been seen in Netherhoughton, hanging about the tobacconist's – but no one who took a look at you could doubt your capabilities.'

Go on then, Fludd silently challenged: look at me. He let his own eyes dwell on the coarse skin of the nun's cheeks, her fleshy nose; she raised her head briefly, but then dropped it again, as if its black wrappings had suddenly become too heavy. She reached out for the teapot and topped up her cup.

'What mess?' Fludd said. 'What are you talking about?'

Perpetua was startled. She put down the pot. 'Well, don't tell me His Grace hasn't put you in the picture? Angwin's to be modernized, he's to be made to change his ways, I thought you knew all that. Perhaps – I don't know – perhaps the bishop thought it would be better if you formed your own opinions. A very fair man, His Grace, a very just man, I always have said that about him. Though in my opinion the benefit of the doubt can be extended once too often.' She thought for a moment, and suddenly sat up straighter, preening herself. 'Of course, he knew that you had a reliable source here. He knew that he could rely on me to set you straight.'

Father Fludd picked up one of Sister Anthony's biscuits. He bit into it, gave a cry of pain, and dropped it to his knee, whence it bounced to the floor and skittered under the table. 'Holy Virgin,' he said. 'I have nearly broke my teeth.'

'Lord, I should have warned you, Father. We are all used to them. We have a little toffee hammer that we pass about to deal with them.'

Fludd held his hand across his mouth.

'Would you like me to look in your mouth?' Perpetua said tenderly. 'I could see if there was any damage.'

'No thank you, Mother Perpetua. Do go on with what you were saying.'

'The man's in a world of his own,' the nun continued. 'More tea? Oh, he's sound enough on doctrine, we all know that, too sound, the bishop says, an obstinate sort of man always on about the Church Fathers and talking over people's heads. But his sermons can be mere gibberish. In the pulpit the other week he said the Pope was a Nazi. He said he was the head of the Mafia.'

'And the congregation?' Fludd took out his handkerchief and dabbed at his lip. 'How did they take it?'

'Quietly,' said the nun, with a careless air. 'They always do. They've a great want of education.'

And whose fault is that? Fludd muttered, behind the muffling folds of linen.

'And if his wild sermons were not offence enough, he sets his judgement up against His Grace's! Of course, you've heard of this ridiculous business about the statues.'

'Oh, of course,' said Fludd. He was beginning to sense which way the wind was blowing. 'I think I will have that other cup of tea.'

By now the scuffling outside the door had much increased, and a sort of impatient rhythmic breathing was evident, the concerted effort of six lungs.

'Oh, come in,' Purpit cried, her patience snapping. 'Don't hang about out there snuffling like a tribe of old dogs, come in and meet Father Fludd, the great hope of our parish.'

The three nuns who entered the room in single file were of an age, as Purpit had told him, and of a height, which was little more than five foot; looking from one lined, dim, paper-white face to the other, Fludd knew that he would never be able to tell them apart. They kept their eyes cast down, behind their wire-framed spectacles, and shuffled their feet. Their habits smelt musty, as if they never went out of doors. Of course, they did go out of doors, walking up and down the carriage-drive; but what they experienced, between the black banks and the dripping trees, did not count as fresh air. They took no exercise, apart from beating small children with canes – which they did fiercely, in a spirit of rivalry. Malice marked their countenances, and a kind of greed.

'Are we not going to have tea?' one of them said. 'The pot is big enough.'

'We could fetch cups,' said another.

'You have had your tea,' said Purpit, crushingly.

The three nuns peered at Fludd, from beneath the starched parapets of their headdresses. 'They are working on a tapestry,' Mother Perpetua said. 'Aren't you, Sister Polycarp?'

'It is a big one,' said Polycarp.

'We do it *ad majorem Dei gloriam*,' said Cyril.

'It is like the Bayeux Tapestry.'

'But on a religious theme.'

Fludd set down his teacup. He felt uneasy; one of the

Sisters wheezed a little, and he felt that his own breathing had become difficult, a pain across his breastbone.

'You don't sound well, Sister,' he said; and he saw the lips of the other two nuns tighten with wrath.

'She is very well,' one said.

The other said, 'She gets linctus.'

The first added, 'She has no cause for complaint.'

'Your tapestry . . .' Fludd said, 'what is the theme?'

'The plagues of Egypt,' said Sister Cyril. 'It is novel.'

'But edifying,' said Polycarp.

'It is an undertaking,' said Fludd, respectfully.

'We have done the plague of frogs,' Polycarp said. 'And the murrain, and the grievous swarm of flies.'

Sister Ignatius Loyola coughed a long hacking cough, then spoke for the first time: 'Now we are up to boils.'

Perpetua took him to the convent door. It was quite dark now, and he knew that Father Angwin would be anxious. Perpetua touched his sleeve. 'Remember, Father,' she said, in a hoarse whisper, 'any help I can give you, you've only to ask. Any information . . . you understand? I want His Grace to know I'm loyal.'

'I understand,' Fludd said. He wondered what exactly was the origin of the bad blood between the nun and Father Angwin; but he had already realized, from what he had seen earlier that day, that the quarrels of this community were ancient and impenetrable. He wanted to get away, out of her presence; a powerful aversion welled up in him, and he pulled his sleeve away. Purpit did not notice. She stood framed in the lighted doorway as he trudged up the hill towards the church.

The bishop's a fair man, he thought; as he put one muddy foot in front of the other. The bishop's a just man, is he? Well, perhaps so. Perhaps he may be. Perhaps fairness abounds. When people complain of their lot, their sneering enemies gloat, and tell them, to make them afraid, 'life's not fair'. But then again, taking the long view, and barring flood, fire, brain damage, the usual run of bad luck, people do get what they want in life. There is a hidden principle of equity in operation. The frightening thing is that life *is* fair; but what we need, as someone has already observed, is not justice but mercy.

Chapter Five

The arrival of Father Fludd in the parish was marked by a general increase in holiness. If he thought his parish tour had gone unremarked, he was mistaken; on the next Sunday, and in subsequent weeks, the lukewarm, the reclusive and the apostate trod in each other's footsteps on the carriage-drive. He preached a good vigorous sermon, stuffed with well-chosen texts; Father Angwin had thought it on the whole dangerous to disabuse his flock of the notion that the Bible was a Protestant book, and had tended to leave his quotes unattributed.

That first Sunday, Fludd noted the Men's Fellowship, occupying the north aisle; a dapper man in plaid trews was the first of them to step up and take Holy Communion, and the rest followed. Their jaws were held stiff as they turned from the altar rail, God's living body cloven to their hard palates. Bestowing the host, Fludd saw the features of the communicants reflected in the polished plate the altar boy held beneath each chin; he saw the shiver of the distorted metal faces.

Only the nuns preceded the Men's Fellowship, Purpiture marching stoutly from her front pew, the rest rising to follow, peeling off from the kneeler like black adhesive strips: Cyril, Ignatius, Polycarp, in alphabetical order to save dispute. The round-faced girl-nun brought up the rear; one or two sisters were absent, he noticed, probably down with some digestive ailment.

A hymn then, 'O Bread of Heaven': off-key, a low rumbling hymn, like bad weather coming up. *Ita, Missa est:* Go, the Mass is ended. *Deo gratias.* Another hymn: 'Soul of My Saviour', a parish favourite. High-pitched, this time, a keening wail, the sopranos of Fetherhoughton having their way with it; only the shrillest can hit the top notes, and the wisest do not try. *Soul of my Saviour, Sanctify my breast* . . . And midway through that first torturing verse, he saw from the corner of his eye how Mother Perpetua leant forward, across the embonpoint of Sister Anthony, and dug the young nun in the ribs.

If she had been carrying an umbrella, she would have used that, but the point of her finger was hardly less efficacious. A startled moan broke from Sister Philomena, and presently it was evident that she was singing. *Deep in thy wounds, Lord, Hide and shelter me* . . . 'Poor Sister Philomena,' Agnes Dempsey muttered. 'It's like a dog being taken poorly.' The young woman blushed as she sang, and cast down her eyes.

When the hymn was over, the congregation rose as one man, and seemed to shake themselves, and passed weightily down the aisles and out into the weak autumn sun, *en route* to their fast-breaking Sunday dinners; the camphor smell of their Sunday clothes mingled with the incense, and Fludd found himself sneezing uncontrollably, wiping his streaming eyes. There was mud on the carriage-drive, and winter in the air.

Soon the children had new games, of imitating priests. In their back-yards they went knocking from door to door, slow-footed and doleful, pretending that they carried the viaticum. The householders, informed that they were near death, made their displeasure felt; but the children, having recovered from the blows, re-formed their lines, and began to visit the coalhouses, tapping on each door to solicit last confessions, and to offer the grace of God to the Nutty Slack within.

Even the people of Netherhoughton came to church, and sat glowering at the back; their little heathen children played in the aisles with their ouija boards.

On the Monday, in the afternoon, Fludd was kneeling in church, praying for Father Angwin. He might have been on the altar, for that was his privilege; but he would rather kneel in the first bench, where the nuns had been on Sunday, and watch from that short distance the sanctuary lamp, winking redly at him like an alcoholic uncle.

He wanted peace of mind for Father Angwin; he thought of the hymn, 'Soul of My Saviour', of how the ignorant parish mangled the words and sense. He thought of the women of Fetherhoughton, slack chins quivering above their buttoned-up coat fronts: *Guard and defend me/From the formaligh* . . . Oh, foe malign, he had breathed, his back to them, his thin hands passing over the sacred vessels; from the foe malign. He had glanced down, sideways, and noticed the altar boys' big black lace-up shoes sticking from beneath their cassocks, and their wrinkly grey wool socks. *In destrier moments, make me only thine* . . . What are they talking about? What do they think they are singing? He pictured the formaligh, a small greasy type of devil with sharp teeth, which lurked on dark nights in the church porch. Of all the small devils, Fludd thought, ignorance is chief of the horde; their misapprehension had embodied it, given it flesh.

Now – Monday, kneeling here alone – he could hear the rain coming down, as hard as on the night he arrived; drumming unseen behind the stained glass, splashing and gurgling from the downspouts, falling alike on the just and the unjust. He closed his eyes, would have closed his ears to shut out the sound, to sink himself into that trance-like state

where he would hear, if God were willing, some small recommendation; some recommendation as to how he should
proceed, as to what, having found this place, he ought to do
next.

Images flitted through his mind: the nine-runged ladder,
the railwayman's kerchief that snapped on its fence pole in
the moorland wind, the black arm of Mother Perpetua
uplifted in the twilight; and Agnes Dempsey, standing inside
the front door mute like a dog, waiting for his return. One by
one the pictures chased each other, and he held open his
mind's door, and let them pass through, until the house was
empty; his pulse slowed, his breathing deepened, the rain
stilled itself to a whisper and faded into a profound silence.

Am I alive? the small voice asked itself. What is, you know
by what is not; for as Augustine says, 'We have some knowledge of the darkness and silence, of the former only by the
eyes, by the latter only through the ears; nevertheless we
have no sensation, only the privation of sensation.' In the
realm of Taut, the underworld of the Egyptians, there were
twelve divisions; one of the twelve was guarded by a serpent
with four legs and a human face. Here the darkness was so
thick that it might be felt; but this is almost the only instance
we have. When we say the night has a velvet darkness, we
romance. When we say the soul is black, we are turning a
phrase.

Now, coming to himself a little, Fludd thought he heard
behind him a ragged breathing; something had come in at the
far door, and stood watching him while he prayed. He did
not turn his head. I am breaking down, he thought, dissolving
into destruction and despair; this is my *nigredo*, this is the
darkest night of my soul. Just as the statues lie in their
shallow graves, taking on the hue of the soil and the smell of
mortification, so my spirit is buried, walled in with corrupt-
ing agents. Agnes had said to him (busy with the kettle, her
face averted, her voice cracking with the strength of her

sentiments), 'When I walk over them, Father, I shudder. We all shudder.' He had said, 'They are symbols, Miss Dempsey. Symbols are powerful things.' Miss Dempsey had said, 'It's like walking on the dead.'

But everything that is going to be purified must first be corrupted; that is a principle of science and art. Everything that is to be put together must first be taken apart, everything that is to be made whole must first be broken into its constituent parts, its heat, its coldness, its dryness, its moisture. Base matter imprisons spirit, the gross fetters the subtle; every passion must be anatomized, every whim submit to mortar and pestle, every desire be ground and ground until its essence appears. After separation, drying out, moistening, dissolving, coagulating, fermenting, comes purification, recombination: the creation of substances that the world has until now never beheld. This is the *opus contra naturem*, this is the spagyric art; this is the Alchymical Wedding.

The creature, behind him, was advancing with a heavy tread, coming up the centre aisle. His hands still clasped before him, he turned and looked over his right shoulder.

It was Sister Philomena, a sack over her head to keep off the rain; her habit was girded up to her knees with an arrangement of string that caught it into sculptural folds.

Father Fludd stared at the nun's feet. She said, 'I've got a dispensation for wellingtons. A special permission, from Mother Provincial. It's always me they send out in the wet, not that I'm complaining, I like to get out. I'm getting a dispensation for a rainmate.'

'What are those?' Fludd said.

'They're plastic hoods that you can put over your head. See-through, they are. When you fold them up you can concertina them as small as that –' she put out her damp fingers, and showed him – 'and put them in your pocket.'

'I hate plastic,' Father Fludd said.

'You would. You're a man.' She corrected herself: 'You're

a priest. You never have to clean. Plastic's easy-clean. You just wipe it. I wish the whole world was made of plastic.'

Philomena emerged into the light, the pool of light cast by the candles that burnt before St Theresa, the Little Flower. 'I see Mother has been up lighting candles,' she said.

'Has she a particular devotion to St Theresa?'

'Well, Theresa was a nun, of course, and she was a very humble sort. Humility was what she specialized in, she was more good at it than anybody in her convent, she was famous for it. Mother reckons we all ought to be that humble. St Theresa went into the convent when she was very young. They weren't going to let her, but she put her foot down about it. They tried to stop her, but she wouldn't take no for an answer. There was no holding her. She complained to the Pope.'

'You must have been studying her life.'

'We have a book in the convent library.'

'Is your library extensive?'

'Well, there's some lives of the saints. Oh, and a *Turf Guide*, that's Sister Anthony's.' Philomena put out her hand and leant heavily on the back of one of the treacle-stained benches. She seemed a little out of breath. 'St Theresa eventually pegged out from her chest, like my Aunt Dymphna. In St Theresa's case it was the penances she used to do that brought it on, but I don't think that was the case with my aunt. Humble to the last, and wanting to offer her mortal agony up as a sacrifice for sinners, the saint refused those medicines that could have relieved her final distress. So the book says. I don't know whether Dymphna was offered any morphine. I expect she took some whiskey.'

Fludd leant backwards, sliding imperceptibly from the kneeler to the bench. He sat looking at the nun. She had taken off her sack and shaken from it a few dead leaves that had fallen on her as she ploughed her way up the carriage-drive. 'I'll pick them up,' she said. 'I'll sweep.' She took out something from her pocket. 'I've come to have another go at the nose,' she said.

Fludd followed her gaze, up to the statue of the Virgin. It seemed a hammer-blow had taken the tip of her nose clean off. 'I did that,' Philomena said. 'It didn't seem reverent altogether, but I needed a flat bit to start with, so I borrowed a chisel from the Men's Fellowship, from Mr McEvoy. The first nose I put on was with modelling clay, and then I thought I could paint it, but of course it would have to be fired first, so that wasn't a success. So now I've been trying with plasticine' – she held it out on the palm of her hand – 'kneading different bits together to try to get the shade.'

'I think she should be darker,' Fludd said. 'Realistically. She came from an eastern land.'

'I can't think the bishop would take to that idea.'

'I have seen black virgins,' Fludd said. 'In France they call them Our Lady *sous-terre*. In their processions, only green candles are burnt.'

'It sounds pagan,' she said doubtfully. 'Will you excuse me, Father? I have to get up there. On that bench.'

'Of course.' He stood up quickly, and moved away. Philomena made a deep genuflection to the altar, then sat down on the bench opposite and began to pull off her wellingtons.

'I would help you, Sister,' Fludd said. 'But. You know.'

'I'll have them off in a minute,' she said, kicking and wrestling. He turned his eyes away. She laughed, grunted and tussled. 'There.' The boots fell over on to the stone flags. Spry and nimble now, she stepped up on to the bench where he had been sitting, and stretched out to reach the Virgin. 'What would you think?' she asked. 'Make the nose first, then slap it on, or try to work it while I'm up here?'

'I think you should model it *in situ*. May I try? I am taller.'

'Hop up then, Father. You will certainly have a longer reach.'

He stepped up on the bench beside her, and she took a

sideways step to accommodate him, then gave him the plasticine from her fingertips. It was the colour of bloodless skin, and cold to the touch; he worked it in the palm of his hand. He faced the Virgin at point-blank range, and stared into her painted blue eyes.

Sister Philomena watched intently as he reached forward, and planted his model on the statue's face. He could feel her attention, fastening on his hand; he could smell the wet serge of her habit, and, when he looked sideways, in an unspoken request for her opinion, he could see the white-blonde down on her cheek. As if to steady herself, she put out a hand to the Virgin's slippery narrow shoulder, and it lay there cold and blue-veined against the blue of the painted cloak.

For a moment, Fludd supported the girl, a hand under her elbow; then he leapt backwards to the floor. He stood off, to consider. 'Not a success,' he said. 'On the whole. Will you come and look?'

'No.' She dropped her eyes, despondent. 'I shall never get it remodelled, not even with your help, Father. We have perfectly good statues, mouldering under the ground.'

He looked up. 'Do you think they are mouldering? You too?'

'Oh, you frighten me.' She touched the black cross that hung on a cord around her neck. 'It was just an expression I used.'

'But *something* is rotten here.'

'Yes. Have you come to help it?'

'I don't know. I think it is beyond me. I think I can only help myself. And make, perhaps, one or two little adjustments in the parish.'

'Can you do anything for me?'

'Come down from there.' He held out his hand. She took it and stepped down, with one neat, stately movement. 'Once,' he said, 'when people made statues, they carved their garments in neat folds, as if there were no body underneath.

Then came a time when ideas changed. Even the saints have limbs, even the Virgin. They began to round out the folds.'

'Our statues looked various. Some lifelike, some dead.'

'I'm afraid none of them were so old that they go back to the time of which I speak. If they did not seem lifelike, it was from lack of skill. Or distaste for flesh.'

'Oh, well.' She looked down, then blushed. She began to fumble and tug at her skirts. 'I didn't think anybody would be in here,' she said. 'I usually kilt up my habit when it rains, only don't tell on me. It gets so miserable when you're muddy round the hem for the rest of the day, it's enough to bring on rheumatics. I don't suppose,' she said, 'that St Theresa would have minded a bit of rain. She'd have offered it up. She'd probably have gone and stood out in it on purpose.'

But when they left the church, they found that the rain had stopped. A weak sunlight, which itself seemed flooded with water, washed the tree trunks of the carriage-drive. Light glazed the puddles, and made them opaque; it seemed that the ground had been set for a banquet, with shallow white china bowls.

That night after dinner, Father Angwin said, 'I have had a call from the bishop.'

'Oh yes?' Fludd said. 'What did he want?'

'He wanted to know if I was relevant.' Father Angwin raised his face to Fludd, expectantly; but it was a barbed expectation. 'You are clever and modern, Father Fludd, can you make anything of that?'

Fludd did not reply; indicating by his silence that he did not mean to be drawn out, about his modernity.

'He said, "Are you relevant, Father? Are you real?" I said, well, that's one for Plato. But the bishop continued without a pause. "Are your *sermons* relevant?" he said. "Are you attuned to the modern ear?"'

'I've never heard anything of this before,' Fludd said. 'Relevant? No, I've not heard of it. What did you say?'

'I said I was supremely bloody irrelevant, if he pleased, and I would, by his leave, remain so – for the welfare of my parishioners, and the salvation of their souls. "Indeed, how so, my dear chap?"' Father Angwin fell to ferocious mimicry, thrusting his legs forward and patting at an imaginary paunch. 'Because, I said, isn't irrelevance what people come to church for? Do you want me to greet them with the language of the tramshed? Do you want me to take such spirituality as they possess and grind it up in the Co-op butcher's mincing-machine?' Father Angwin looked up, his eyes alight. 'To that, he made no answer.'

'I hope you seized your advantage,' said Father Fludd.

'Well, while I had him on the hop, I raised the matter of my statues again. If saints, I said, will not come to Fetherhoughton, may I not have their mute representatives? Are they not the spurs to faith, and is not faith my business, and are the statues not then the tools of my trade? I said to him, why do you take away the tools of my trade? Would you deprive the physician of his black bag? May a barber not have his pole?'

'Where does the bishop think the statues are?' Fludd asked carefully.

'Oh, he thinks I have them in my garage.'

'And would he concede anything at all?'

'Nothing.'

'And so how did you leave it?'

'I said, I hope I live to bury you.' Father Angwin brooded for a moment. 'He didn't mention you.'

'Oh well,' said Fludd. 'Did he not? Never mind.'

Father Angwin still half-believed, when he thought about it, that Fludd was the bishop's spy. But he conceived that even the bishop must have a better nature, which made him tactfully gloss over the fact of the spy's existence, as if he could not quite admit to what he had done. Either that, or his left hand knows not what his right hand is doing.

Father Angwin, of course, was the worse for drink. Father Fludd gently pointed this out to him, and went into the kitchen to get Agnes to make him some coffee. Coffee was an innovation, one that he was working on. You grind, Miss Dempsey. You measure. You moisten. You heat. You filter. Well, Miss Dempsey would say, I don't know what the result will be; it will be a substance I have never beheld before.

Father Angwin, left alone, looked into the fire in a dream. Earlier that evening, he had listened to a most peculiar confession: or rather, to a question put to him in the confessional, by a strange, strained voice, that he believed he had heard somewhere, but could not quite place. It had been Netherhoughton night; a special evening was reserved for the people from up the hill. It had been in his mind to send Fludd, but the curate wasn't up in their ways yet; either none of them would come at all, or there would be three or four of them trying to get into the box together, all of them fighting to get their version in first. More than once it had degenerated into brawls; the boy was able for that sort of thing, no doubt, he was a strong-looking lad, but discretion is the better part of valour, and he might not have the wit to forestall trouble.

The penitent, first of the evening, had come shuffling into the box, and had knelt, and kept silence, as if waiting for him to speak first. After a while, it had occurred to him that this was some Netherhoughtonian who had come back to church after twenty or thirty years, hoping that the new priest was a soft touch, and who did not know where to begin on his or her sins, and who might anyway have forgotton the usual form of words. Encouragingly, he prompted: 'Bless me, Father, for I have sinned . . .?'

At the sound of his voice there was a small sigh, and a further silence. He waited. It was clear to him that the

Netherhoughtonian had hoped for Fludd. 'Well, now you're here,' he said, 'you may as well get on. Don't worry, I'll help you out. Why not take it a decade at a time? But first, tell me, how long is it since your last confession?'

'Not long,' the penitent said flatly. It was a woman; her age he could not guess. And what she said might be true, in the Netherhoughtonian perception. Up there, they were still gossiping about the Abdication; not that of Edward VIII, but that of James II. Their quarrels stretched back to time immemorial; they had grievances that pre-dated the Conquest.

'Well,' the voice said; and there was a further pause. 'Well, I've nothing to tell, really. I could ask you a question.'

'All right. Your question then.'

'Would it be a sin for a man to set fire to his house?'

Now this was the kind of rough, wild stuff you got from the folk of Netherhoughton. 'His own house?' the priest asked. 'You don't mean someone else's?'

'His own,' said the voice impatiently. 'If he is poor, and the insurance money would put him in better circumstances.'

'Oh, I see. Well, of course it would be a sin.' Father Angwin thought, I did not know that in Netherhoughton they had insurance, if I were a company I would refuse them. 'It's a crime besides. Arson, and fraud. Oblige me by putting the notion out of your head.'

'All right,' the penitent said, taking his point with surprising alacrity. 'I could put another question. May dripping be used for pastry, or is it allowed only for frying fish?'

God help them, Father Angwin thought; accustomed as they are to living on gruel, shall I live to see the day when their tastes are broadened, their puny physiques improved? 'I can't tell you, right off. But,' he said helpfully, 'I could ask my housekeeper. Why don't I do that, and you could come back next week, and hear the answer? I'm sure that if you're struggling she'd be willing to give you many hints and tips in the culinary line.'

A pause. 'No,' the voice said. 'Fasting and abstinence. That's what I'm talking about. Lenten regulations. And on a Friday through the year. Does dripping count as meat? Or does it count as butter?'

'That's a tough one,' the priest said. 'Let me think about it, will you?'

'Can you have jam on a fast day?'

'I always do, if I want. I don't believe there's an ordinance about it. You must be governed by the general principles, though. You mustn't be a glutton for jam.'

'If it is a fast day, and you are taking your morning collation, eight ounces of bread that is, can the bread be toasted?'

'Oh yes, it may.'

'But then it would shrink up, Father. Perhaps it might weigh less. So you could have an extra slice.'

'I don't think there's anything in Canon Law about that.' He was concerned; and puzzled too, by the scruple and lack of scruple this penitent combined. 'Do you get very hungry on fast days? There are some people who do. I believe that all but the most rigid authorities will allow a little more in cases of hardship.'

'I should not want to put myself forward as such a case.'

'Your efforts do you credit.'

'But now tell me, Father, how long has it been permitted to eat meat on Christmas Day, when Christmas Day falls on a Friday?'

'Since 1918, I think you will find,' Father Angwin said readily. 'Since the new code of Canon Law came in, at Pentecost that year.'

'And what date did Pentecost fall?'

'I believe it was 19 May.'

'Thank you. And on a Friday, or other day of abstinence . . . is turtle soup permitted?'

'I rather think so,' Father Angwin said. 'Are you accustomed to turtle soup?'

'No,' said the penitent, with more than a tinge of regret. 'Well, thank you, Father, you've cleared up a couple of points that have been bothering me. Any further thoughts on the dripping?'

'If I had to give an answer – off the top of my head mind – I'd say dripping may be used for both purposes. But I will certainly look into it. And if you care to come back, you shall have chapter and verse on it.'

He wanted to say, who are you? There seemed something forced about the penitent's husky voice; its rough-and-ready tone, that way of shuttling on from one question to the next, bespoke a certain familiarity, although the people of Nether-houghton were no respecters of persons. He couldn't place it. Yet it was as if the penitent knew his foibles, and divined his motto: fidelity in small things.

'You will come again, won't you?' he said wistfully; he had enjoyed the questions about dietary laws.

'Mm,' the penitent said.

'Is there anything else? Something you have to tell me?'

'No.'

'You know, I can't give you absolution. You haven't con-fessed.'

'I can't confess,' the voice said. 'I hardly know nowadays if things are sins or not. And if I did, and they were, perhaps I shouldn't be sorry.'

'You don't need Perfect Contrition,' Father Angwin said. (He must instruct his penitent; Father Fludd had opined that it was the spell-book, not the catechism, that they used in Netherhoughton.) 'Imperfect Contrition will do. That is the kind of contrition,' he explained, 'that arises out of fear of Hell, rather than love of God. Don't you fear Hell?'

A pause. A whisper. 'Very much.'

'And then you must have a Firm Purpose of Amendment. That means, you know, that you must really sincerely make your mind up you're not going to do it again. And then I can absolve you.'

'But I haven't done it,' the voice said. 'I haven't done anything. Not even once. Not yet.'

'But you are contemplating a particular sin?'

'Well, I don't know whether it's in me. I haven't had the chance to find out.'

'You mustn't test yourself,' Father Angwin said. 'You mustn't test yourself against the delights of evil. It's a test you will always pass.'

There was a longer pause. 'Who knows,' said the impenitent penitent, 'what any of us may come to, in the space of a month or two?'

No one else had been at confession tonight. And now, staring into the fire, with the whisky between himself and the occasion, Father Angwin knew perfectly well who his penitent had been. Netherhoughton had been a red herring; this was closer to home. He wondered if she had found any comfort in talking to him, although it was not who she expected. Perhaps she will come again, he thought. We can joust on any topic. Circumlocution has its uses. We shall get to what matters in the end.

He heard Father Fludd's footsteps in the passage. The aroma of fresh coffee wafted through the half-open door.

'You must fast,' Sister Philomena said. Her voice was very clear; carrying to the naughty, scuffling children, those who sat in the back row. 'Before you take communion, you must fast. You mustn't have your breakfast that day. But then when you get home you can have your Sunday dinner.'

It was ten o'clock in the morning. The lights were on. The rain came down outside. The children near the radiators had a baked smell coming from them. Their wellington boots stood tenantless along the far wall; they swung their feet, woollen sausages of sock extending six inches beyond their toes.

The children were almost seven years old. She was preparing them. Next spring they would go to confession for the first time – she would lead them up to the church on a Friday morning – and on the Sunday following they would make their first communion. She wondered if there was anything they could do, between Friday and Sunday, to make a mess of her efforts. How can you tell if they are in mortal sin? You can't keep them in your pockets. Philomena was no sentimentalist; she knew what they were capable of. Great sins, of violence and uncharity, were open to them now; as adults, they would find their range smaller.

A child put up his hand. 'If we only have to fast for three hours, Sister, couldn't we have us breakfasts if we got up very early?'

'You could. It might not be good for your digestion, eating at such an hour.'

'What if I did get up though, Sister, and had us breakfast, and then I found out that us clock was wrong? Mustn't I go to communion that day?'

'Well, if it was a genuine mistake . . .' The children flustered her. 'I don't know,' she said. 'I will ask Father Angwin.' Or I might look it up in my question-and-answer book, she thought. What is time, anyway? The book went on about real times and mean times; it made reference to meridians. It talked about deductions for summer time, and indicated the good practice for people who went by sundials. 'It's to do with Greenwich,' she said. 'All would be well if you were right by Greenwich.'

'Is Greenwich like Lourdes?' they said, putting up their hands. 'Is there cures? Is there miracles there?'

Philomena found the children difficult: more difficult week by week. Perpetua said that the sacrament worked of itself. They didn't have to understand; she, Philomena, was only required to see that they could go through the motions.

'What if I'm doing the fast,' one said, 'and my tooth comes out, and I swallow it?'

'That would just be a little accident,' Philomena said. 'You could still take the sacrament.'

'But Sister, you said we wasn't to touch the host with us teeth. When it was in your stomach –'

From the next classroom, she heard Perpetua's voice raised. She knew the signs and symptoms; soon she would have her cane out.

'What if I'm doing the fast, and a fly flies down us throat?'

'That'll do now,' she said. 'There's plenty of time for the answers to these questions. Now we're going to get up very quietly' – from us desks, she nearly said – 'from our desks, and form a line to put on our wellingtons, and then we're going to form up two by two and walk up to church and have a Holy Communion practice.'

Up to church. Oh God, oh God, she thought, feeling her heart beat faster. What her heart chose to do was nothing she could control; let it thump away and batter and lurch at her ribs, like a puppy locked in a barn. There was no door she could open to let it free.

The mournful crocodile, up the hill and into the church; whispers stilled in the porch, an epidemic of shushing. 'They are so slow,' Purpit had said. 'We must rehearse them all winter for communion in spring. Otherwise they will be blundering into each other and goodness knows what all.' She had offered Philomena the use of her most formidable cane, but the young nun had declined. She knew, perfectly well, that Purpit would like to use it on her.

If only there were a bit of light in the place, she thought. The children's skinny shapes passed into the benches like a file of ghosts, like the ghosts from some children's hospital, an empty fever ward. She picked up a fistful of candles from the Little Flower's box, lit them from those that were burning, and juggled them into their holders. 'Now,' she said. 'Begin.'

At once, and all together, the children leapt up from their kneelers, tripping over each others' legs, scrabbling for the centre aisle. 'Stop, stop, stop,' Philomena yelled. 'Back, back, back. As you were. Kneel down. Close your eyes. Join your hands. When I give the word, first child stand up, walk, second child stand up, walk. Follow on in a line. First child turn left, second child follow, all children follow. Get to the altar rail and kneel down reverently. Join your hands, close your eyes, wait your turn for the Holy Eucharist. When the altar rail is all filled up, children behind stop, there, just there, d'you see, at the top of the aisle. You people that are waiting, don't crowd up behind the people at the rail. Keep a distance. Or however will they get back when they're finished?'

At first they tended to close their eyes at the wrong time, and bump into each other, but after a half hour you could see that they were beginning to get the idea. They knelt at the altar rail with their mouths open, and at the word of command they closed them and paused for a reverent moment, and then rose to stamp back to their places. The signs of strain were evident on their faces. She was not so old that she had forgotten what troubled them. Will you find your place again in the crowded church at eleven o'clock Mass? Will you struggle into the wrong bench, so that people will laugh and point? Will you (worse) attempt to get back down the wrong aisle, and lose your bearings completely? How will you inch and scramble out of your place at the start, without bruising the shins of non-communicants? Will you fit smoothly into the shuffling stream, or somehow hold up the proceedings?

'You must keep your eyes open,' she advised them. 'No, what I mean is, you must keep your wits about you, keep a look-out. The woman on the end of your row, now suppose she's wearing a funny hat. Take a good look at that hat as you go up. Then when you turn from the altar, use it to navigate by.'

She stood at the back of the church, looking up the centre aisle, to judge if the traffic flow was smooth. Her back was to St Thomas Aquinas, the cold saint with his plaster star, and from that direction (as if behind the statue, as if beneath it) she heard a whisper, a rustle, like the feet of a family of mice. Beneath her veil, the hairs pricked at the back of her neck. Then she felt eyes resting on her. She knew it was Fludd. His scrutiny seemed to pass through her black veil, through her starched white under-veil, through her draw-string cap, and revel in what hair she had left these days, and play along her scalp. 'Once more,' she called. 'Eyes closed now. Heads down. Say a little prayer. When I give the word, begin . . . Now.'

She waited only long enough to see the first child, the second child, on their feet and embarked on their march. Then she turned urgently. 'Father? Father?'

Fludd lurked behind the statue. He would not advance. She heard the children, in their wellington boots, clumping towards the altar. She took a step or two, almost running, to the back of the church and the deep shadows under the gallery. 'Are you there?' she whispered. 'Mother Perpetua has taken me off being sacristan. She saw us, the other day, when we were mending the nose. She's in a rage with me for monopolizing your time. I want to talk to you. There are some things I must ask you.'

'Yes,' Fludd said. It was as if the Angelic Doctor had spoken; Fludd's black form could hardly be discerned.

'At the allotments,' she said. 'There's a shed . . .' She could hear the first batch of children now, shuffling back into their places. Too quick, she thought. They should have spent more time at the altar, their knees have barely touched the ground. And feeling these moments of her life begin to slip away, she launched herself forward and clung to the statue's base, to the unyielding plaster hem of the robes, reached out her blue-veined hand and knotted her fingers between the point of the star. Fludd saw her clinging, like a drowning woman to jetsam. He wanted to step forward, but held himself back. His eyes rested upon her. In destrier moments, he thought. In death's drear moments. Make me only thine.

Chapter Six

Outside the purlieus of the convent Philomena had a different kind of walk. She strode ahead of him, swinging her arms carelessly, hopping over the tussocks of grass.

'I came up here one day last year.' The wind scattered her voice. 'Quite early ... it would be April. There were daffodils. Small ones, wild. Not those big yellow brutes you get in the shops.'

Tramping after her, Fludd imagined these blooms. He saw them flinching from the spring winds: frail and whitish yellow, like Chinese hands in sleeves. 'Last year, or this year? I thought last year you weren't here?'

She stopped, catching her breath. 'This year is what I meant. Dear Lord, the months have dragged past. The days seem so long, Father Fludd. They seem to be stretching themselves out. I don't know when that started. I think it was since we buried the statues.'

'I do not find it so,' Fludd said. He felt old, and breathless from the uphill climb, and weary from thankless enterprises. '"My days have passed more swiftly than the web is cut by the weaver, and are consumed without any hope."'

The girl did not recognize a quotation. 'Have you no hope?' She looked up at him for a second. Her eyes were extraordinary, he thought: a smoky fawn flecked here and there with yellow, a colour more suitable in a cat than a nun.

The question seemed to have struck her. Rather than give an answer, Fludd walked on.

'Are you not afraid to be seen?' he asked. 'I doubt you should be here. I may walk where I please, but not you. This is a strange place for a spiritual conference.'

'I came to confession. Netherhoughton night. I thought you would be there. It was the old fellow. I had to hold his attention with some questions about Lent.'

'I have heard a thing about you.'

She turned. Because of her headdress a full turn of her head was necessary, if she were to meet his eyes, and he saw how this fact laid a veneer of import over every exchange. 'The stigmata?'

They had reached the shed of which she had spoken. Its broken door flapped. On the floor were wood-shavings, and the chalky droppings of long-dead fowl.

'Yes,' Fludd said. He ducked his head under the lintel. Inside he had just room to stand upright. A draught, blowing straight from Yorkshire, was unimpeded by the broken window.

Philomena followed him in, ducking her head in turn. 'T'wasn't true,' she said.

'But you pretended it was?'

Philomena looked at her surroundings without contempt. 'I don't care where I come,' she said, 'to get an hour out of that place. People think a convent's quiet, don't they? They should hear Perpetua, going on all day.' She cast around, and leant against a kind of rough workbench, folding her arms. 'I had no choice, you see. They gave me none. Father Kinsella got my mother in on it. You'd have thought they'd got all their birthdays at once.'

'What was it really, if it was not the stigmata?'

'Nerves.'

'What had you to be nervous about?'

'It's a long story. It's about my sister.'

Fludd leant against the wall. He wished he might have a cigarette; it would have been a natural thing. 'Tell it then. Since we are here.'

'Well, she – my sister – came in the convent just after me. Kathleen was her name at home but Finbar was her name in religion. She never said she had a vocation, you know, but my mother's burning ambition was to have us all in the convent, she didn't somehow take to the idea of sons-in-law, and being a grandma and all. At least, that's what we used to say, we girls, and that she wanted to get in with the priest, and have people pointing at her after Mass on a Sunday, saying, "Oh, could you credit that woman's sacrifice, all her daughters given to religion."'

'You had no brother?'

'No. Or he could have been a priest, and perhaps she might not have been so hot on us. One priest in a family equals three or four nuns. That's the way they count in Ireland.'

'So your sister Kathleen entered without a vocation. And it went wrong.'

'She disgraced herself.' Sister Philomena picked up a fold of her habit and ran it between her fingers. She too wished she had, not a cigarette, but something to occupy her, something to distract her from the moment, the place, the person. 'And after she disgraced herself, we got a bad name in the neighbourhood. When I came out in the rash, my mother thought we were going to recoup our fortunes. She was a cleaner, you know, up at the convent, did their shopping for them. I was never away from her a day until I came here. As soon as she noticed it, this thing on my hands, she hauled me off to Father Kinsella, my feet didn't touch the ground.' She imitated her mother's ingratiating mode, her semi-genuflection. '"Look at this, Father, appeared last Friday on Sister Philomena, the very spit and image of the nail marks in the palms of Our Blessed Lord."'

Fludd folded his arms, in a judicious way. 'But what did your sister Kathleen do, to disgrace herself in the first place?'

'She was only just the victim of a muddle. She wasn't a bad-hearted girl at all. Only a novice when the whole thing occurred. In some Orders the novices are kept shut up and taught theology, but in our Order they are set the dirty jobs. When I was a novice I didn't learn much about the spiritual life. I spent the time peeling potatoes. It was more like the army.'

'Was Kathleen – Sister Finbar – was she a rebel?'

'Oh, nothing of that sort. But you know, Father, how nuns can't travel alone? Well, there was a Sister Josephine, a cross old creature with short sight and bad legs, and she got sent to another of the Order's houses, a few miles away. The Order does that, especially when you've been settled about fifty years, they like to put you on general post before you die. Well, our Kathleen – Sister Finbar – was to go with her. Kathleen delivered her safe and sound, but then she had to get back to where she came from. So another sister, Sister Gertrude, she had to escort her, didn't she?'

'Yes, I see a difficulty looming,' said Fludd.

'But when Kathleen got back to her own convent, there was Sister Gertrude, wasn't she? Now, who was to take Gertrude back where *she* belonged?'

Fludd thought about it. 'Kathleen.'

'I see you've a quick grasp of these matters. I suppose some other mind, like Mother Provincial say, might have cut through the difficulty. But Kathleen's superior wasn't any great thinker.'

'What happened then?'

'Our Kathleen took Gertrude back to Gertrude's convent. She asked if she could stay a day or two while she thought it out, but they couldn't have that, they didn't have a permission for it, so they turned her round and sent her straight back again, and another nun with her – Sister Mary Bernard, I think it was.'

'They changed the personnel, but failed to grapple with the principle.'

'Now it was Sister Mary Bernard that was at the wrong end of things. Our Kathleen escorted her back. By this time after all the travelling she was fit to drop. The soles of her shoes were worn thin. When she had handed Sister Mary Bernard over she was hanging about in the parlour, waiting to see who was going to bring her back home this time, and her nerves just snapped. She ran out of the front door.'

'What? She just bolted, did she?'

'She couldn't take it one more time, she said. She knew if they saw her they'd call her back and send somebody with her. So she got over a gate and legged it across the fields. When she came out on to the road she walked along a bit, then she saw a lorry coming. The driver stopped and asked her was she lost or what. He said, hop up here beside me, Sister, and I'll take you where you want to go, so she did. He was a good sort, she said, a real gentleman. He gave her half this cheese sandwich that he'd got for his dinner – she was starving, you see, because she'd always arrived in places at the wrong time for a collation, and in a convent you can only eat at the set times. This man, this lorry driver, he went out of his way for her, took her back to her own convent, right to the door. But when she rolled up, I'm afraid they were anything but pleased to see her.'

'It was innocent,' Fludd said. 'I'm sure it was. The girl was desperate.'

'The lorry driver turned out to be a Protestant, that was what made it worse.'

'The whole thing could have been avoided,' Fludd said, 'if the original sister had only set out with two escorts, instead of one.'

'That would have been reasonable.' Sister Philomena looked gloomy. 'But then, the whole process was very far from reason.'

'So what happened to Kathleen? Did they throw her out?'

'Oh, she got her marching orders all right. They had her out of there before the evening collation – booted out on an empty stomach again, she said, that's what made her bitter. She didn't even get to say goodbye to me. To me, her own sister.'

'What did she do then?'

'She had to go home. My mother couldn't hold her head up in the parish. Soon after that Kathleen went to the bad. Like Aunt Dymphna. Drinking and going to dances. She talked about having her hair bleached, my mother said.' She looked up at him, her face puzzled. 'It's something in our family, I think. Hot blood.'

'Would you mind if I smoked a cigarette, Sister?' Fludd reached for his silver case. He must have something to do. 'I can imagine the effect all this must have had on you.'

'Soon afterwards my hands broke out. I believed it myself, not that I would have shown anybody if it had been left up to me. Is a stigmatic a good person, that's what I wondered. A stigmatic could be the greatest crook.' She looked up. 'Yes, smoke away, I don't mind. Well, it was a nine-days' wonder, my stigmata. The bishop took a dim view of it, they won't hear of miracles nowadays. That's how I came to be here. Tossed out of believing Ireland to this God-forsaken place.'

'You were harshly dealt with. When one considers, say, how much of the mystic vision may be put down to temporal-lobe epilepsy.'

'To what, Father?'

'When St Teresa of Avila had her three day vision of Hell, she was merely working up to a fit ... the flames and the stench were a part of her aura. And the Blessed Hildegard, seeing God's fortress – she was having a migraine attack.'

She looked dubious. 'I don't have fits. I have thin skin. That's all.'

'You don't have as much between you and the world as other people do. Let me see your hand, please.'

She raised one, shaking back her sleeve, and stared fixedly at the palm: as if here, a year on, the delicate embroidery of blood might seep through the skin. Father Fludd leaned forward and reached for her hand with his, as tentative as a cat. He placed the tip of his index finger on to the tip of her second finger. Her outstretched hand, palm upturned, dipped towards him. 'Why are you doing that?' she asked. She too gazed down at her palm. 'You look as if you were going to tell my fortune. But it's forbidden.'

'I could tell your fortune,' Fludd said.

'I tell you,' she said quietly, 'the Church forbids it.'

Fludd touched her forefinger. 'This is the finger of Jupiter,' he said. 'The Ram governs the tip; the middle phalange is governed by Taurus the Bull, and the base by Gemini. This, now,' he took her middle finger, 'is the finger of Saturn. The Goat governs its tip. Here in the middle comes the Water Carrier, then the Fishes. Your third finger is the finger of Apollo, God of the Sun. The Crab governs here, then the Lion, then the Virgin. Venus rules the thumb; the little finger is ruled by Mercury. Libra the Scales governs its tip, Scorpio its middle phalange, the Archer its base.'

'What does it all mean, Father?'

'God knows,' Fludd said. Her lifeline was long and unbroken, curling out of sight into her snug inner sleeve; the Mount of Venus was large and fleshy. He saw a nature active, mutable, fiery; a rationalist's finger-tips. There were no shipwrecks in her palm, no danger from four-legged beasts, or iron instruments; but danger from the malice of women, and from self-doubt, and faintness of heart. 'The line of Saturn is doubled,' he said. 'You will wander from place to place.'

'But I never go anywhere.'

'I am not known to be wrong.'

'It's only an old gypsy thing, anyway.'

'I must differ. This science was practised before gypsies were thought of.'

'Well, if you know so much . . . aren't you going to tell me what's there?'

Fludd lifted his eyes to her face for a second, then dropped them again to her palm. He traced the course of her heartline; it dipped sharply, and ended in a five-pointed star. 'Anything I say is superfluous,' he said. 'The point is, Sister, you know what your fortune will be.'

She drew back her hand. Smiled. Held it splayed and self-conscious against her thigh; hardly touching the cloth of her habit, as if she thought it was smeared with ink. She looked around again. 'I wish we could sit down. I should have thought about it, I could have brought sacks for the floor.' Her foot scraped at the wood-shavings; her words were aimless, random, without meaning.

'You asked me if I could do anything for you. What is it you want?'

She would not look at him; continued that little sidetrack-ing motion with her foot. 'Answers to my questions.'

'About Lent?'

'No.'

'Good. I didn't become a priest to answer that sort of question. I want to answer something deeper.'

She glanced up, just for a moment. 'One of the children asked me, what was there before Creation?'

Cigarette in hand, Fludd looked out of the broken window, beyond the rotting coops and the scraps of chicken wire, to where the railwayman's handkerchief snapped and lashed against its pole. 'There was the *prima materia*, without dimension or quality, neither large nor small, without proper-ties or inclinations, neither moving nor still.'

'I'm afraid they won't take that kind of answer.'

He put his cigarette to his lips. 'What kind of answer do they want?'

'They go on about guardian angels,' she said. 'They expect to be able to see them, walking behind them up the carriage-drive. They think if they could turn round fast enough, they would catch them.'

'Ah,' Fludd said, 'if only any of us could turn round fast enough. We might catch a glimpse of our own face.'

'They say – the children – people are getting born and dying all the time, so you need more and more angels, or after somebody's died do they get reassigned? They say, what if you die young, does your angel get forty years off? One of them said last week, my guardian angel used to be Hitler's.'

'Angels aren't following us,' Fludd said. 'No one's following us, except ourselves. Look at you. They sent you out from Ireland. Are you less tormented now? No. Yourself followed you.'

'I have to teach them the Creed. I have problems there. Jesus was crucified, and then, it says, "he descended into Hell".'

'Limbo, is meant,' said Fludd; taking the orthodox line.

'Yes, I know. That's what I was always taught.'

'But you don't believe it?'

'Why should he go to Limbo? Just a lot of old patriarchs and prophets, and little dead babies nobody had time to baptise. I like to think it is really Hell that is meant. I like to think of him paying a call. To be reacquainted with it.' Fludd raised an eyebrow. 'Reacquainted,' she said. 'After all, he made it.'

The air about them was growing colder now, light fading from the sky; he had never known evening come down so early as it did among these hills. The girl's eyes had lost their daytime glow; they looked slaty now, a Fetherhoughton colour. He shivered a little, dropped his cigarette end on to the floor, put his hands in his pockets.

'I was thinking,' Philomena said, 'why does God permit the bishop to exist?'

'It's more than a permission. God made him.'

'He's gross. He's like a pork-butcher.'

'You could ask, why did God make anything that doesn't please us? But he does not have the same sensibilities as we do. He does not share our tastes.'

'Why did God let my Aunt Dymphna and my sister Kathleen go to the bad?'

'Perhaps he did not take a special interest in undoing them. Perhaps they undid themselves. You said they had hot blood.'

'Will Dymphna roast in Hell for all eternity? Or can it have an end? We are not allowed, are we, to pray for the people in Hell?'

'Not under normal circumstances. Though they say that Gregory the Great prayed out the Emperor Trajan. And we think of Origen's doctrine of Larger Hope ... It was his belief that all men will ultimately be saved. Eternity isn't really exactly that. The torment of Hell is a purifying process, and there will be an end to our punishment.'

She glanced up, half-hoping. 'Is that a respectable belief?'

'No. Most people think that Origen got his wires crossed.'

'Because it occurs to me ... if Hell has an end, does Heaven?' She stopped scraping the ground with her foot, came over to stand by him and look out of the broken window. 'Are these the sort of questions you became a priest to answer?'

Fludd shivered. 'I wish I had a hip-flask.'

'I fancied it was growing warmer.'

'Is it?' His eyes opened wide. He seemed taken aback; he looked away, and seemed to mutter something to himself. He touched the shed's wall, gingerly, as if fire might have begun in the damp fibres of the wood. Can it be, he thought, that the transformative process is already underway? In these days, he no longer worked in metal, but practised on human nature; an art less predictable, more gratifying, more dangerous. The scientist burns up his experimental matter in the *athenor*, or furnace, but no scientist, however accomplished, can light that furnace himself. The spark must be set by a shaft of celestial light; and in waiting for that light, a man could waste his life. 'It is warmer,' he said, aloud. 'I dare say the wind has dropped.'

The girl stared out at it, riffling the twilit grass. Her cheeks glowed. She knew it was no use to look around her for the source of heat; it was inward. Since he came here, she thought, a match had been put to her future. She did not think she loved him, but still, something burned: a slow, white flicker of approaching change.

'Well, tell me,' she said. 'What made you enter the priesthood, Father?'

'There are some men,' Fludd said, 'who are driven to be surgeons. From an early age they have an appetite to slit up persons and look into their guts. Some men are so consumed by it, that if want of money or education impedes them from obtaining the qualifications they desire, they will simply impersonate surgeons. Many an appendix has been whipped out, in our major hospitals, by some fellow who's walked in off the street.'

She was impressed. 'Wouldn't you ever think they'd be found out? Wouldn't you ever think they'd kill somebody?'

'Sometimes they do. But not more than their quota.'

Jesus, she thought. In England they have a quota. 'So they get away with it, you're saying?'

'Sometimes for years. But then you know there are other men, the would-be priests, they have a complementary desire; they want to take a scalpel to the soul. Sin is their intestinal loops. You can see them drape it around their hands as they go probing into the depths.'

His language was not strange to her. Each morning as she ate her breakfast she regarded the neat antiseptic wounds of Christ. *One of the soldiers with a spear opened his side, and immediately there came out blood and water.* 'But it's not quite the same as doctors,' she said. 'You can't cure sin, can you?'

'The physicians can't cure a half of the corporeal diseases that they go after. They only do it out of curiosity, and to keep the patients' relatives satisfied, and to earn a crust.'

The temperature around her seemed to have increased now. Why did he not feel it? It was a Mediterranean frenzy of heat, a Sicilian afternoon. The wool of her undergarments fretted her skin, and she felt a heat-rash prickle between her shoulder-blades and along her forearms. She said, 'Father Fludd, you're not a real priest, are you? I thought it all along.'

Fludd didn't answer. He might well not answer, she thought. But his features seemed less pinched now; the warmth had touched even his usual corpse-like pallor. 'In my former trade,' he said, 'a trade which I seem to have forgotten now, or at least I have lost my touch with it, there was a business which we called the *nigredo*, which is a process of blackening, of corruption, of mortification, of break-down. Then there is a process we call the *albedo*, it is a whitening . . . Do you see?'

She seemed afraid; looking at him with her eyes large, her expression drawn. 'What is that trade?'

'It was a deep science,' he said. 'Releasing spirit from matter. It should be every man's study.'

'A killer does it. When he kills. Is that a deep science?'

'There are things in one's self one must kill.'

'Oh, I know,' she said wearily. 'The flesh and its appetites. I have been hearing it since I was seven. I am sick of hearing it. Don't you start.'

'I meant something else really. I meant that there are times in life when you must murder the past. Take a hatchet to what you used to be. Axe down the familiar world. It's hard, very painful, but it is better to do it than to keep the soul trapped in circumstances it can no longer abide. It may be that we had a way of life that used to satisfy us, but it does so no more; or a dream which has soured by long-keeping, or a pleasure which has become a habit. Outworn expectations, Sister, are a cage in which the soul rots away, like a mangy beast in a menagerie. When the reality in our head and the reality in the world are at a disjunction, we feel pained, fretted –' He broke off and stared at her, at the crucifix on her chest, the serge and flannel behind it, the epidermis behind that; and she felt her skin crawl, itch, flame. 'Fretted,' he said, sucking his lip. 'Irritated. Itching. Flayed. Besides, I'm not sure about this killing the flesh. We have a saying, *If it were not for the earth in our work, the air would fly away, neither would the fire have its nourishment, nor the water its vessel.*'

'Those are lovely words,' she said. 'Like a psalm. You weren't some kind of Protestant, were you? A lay-preacher?'

'I think we must accommodate our bodies, you know. I think we must find some good in them. Otherwise, as you say, the most blessed men would be the executioners. Besides, grace perfects nature. It doesn't destroy it.'

'Who says so?'

'Um,' Fludd said, unwilling to name-drop. 'St Thomas Aquinas.'

She put out a hand: that palm on which he had already seen the star of a happy destiny. 'Oh, him,' she said. She smiled slowly. She reached out, touched his shoulder. 'Him,' she said. 'He was always a friend of mine.'

She hoped the warmth would follow them, out into the evening; but Fludd had become cold and silent, and the hand he offered to steady her over the rough ground hardly seemed to be the hand of a human being, so spare and chilly was the flesh. The wind rushed the clouds across the chimneys of Fetherhoughton, down below them; she looked up at the black wild jut of moorland, and felt suddenly sobered, and afraid.

She let the priest – the man – tow her along; he seemed to know the way, although he was a stranger to the district, and if he had walked the allotments in the daylight it could not have been more than a half a dozen times. He turned without faltering on to the convent path. He must eat a lot of carrots, she thought; can see in the dark.

'The stile,' Fludd said. 'Just ahead of us now. Can you manage?'

They reached it; he mounted first. Philomena was half over, putting out her long leg in its thick fuzzy stocking. A shape materialized: from, it seemed, the ditch.

'Good evening,' Fludd said. 'Mr McEvoy, isn't it?'

She imagined, though she could not see, that the parishioner gave him a look: as if to say, yes, young fellow, you will learn who I am. But when McEvoy approached, and took out a pocket torch, and shone it, his face wore its normal expression, amiable but knowing.

'Taking my constitutional,' he explained.

'In the dark?'

'It is my habit,' said McEvoy. 'I seem, Father, better equipped than you and Sister Philomena, although by venturing the observation I mean no breath of criticism. Would you care to borrow my pocket torch?'

'Father Fludd can see in the dark,' she said.

'Handy,' said McEvoy. His tone was sardonic. His torch beam travelled downwards; it came to rest on her leg, and slithered over it, as if her stocking had fallen down.

'Come, Sister,' Fludd said. 'Don't stick there. Hop over.' He held out his hand; but the tobacconist was there before him, courtly but insistent. 'I should never like to see a Sister struggle,' McEvoy said. 'You will find me always at your service, a strong arm and a willing heart.'

He seemed to know it was effusive, uncalled-for; backed away under Fludd's sharp look, and then touched his cap. His exit was as sudden as his entrance: sucked away into the murk.

She shuddered. 'Father Angwin says he is the devil.'

Fludd was surprised. 'McEvoy? Why, but he's a harmless man.'

She felt the distance between them increase; a shaft of cold, as he moved from her side.

'Has Father Angwin never spoken to you of it? Of meeting him one afternoon?'

'Yes. He has spoken of something of that kind. But he did not say the man's name.'

'I don't know why he thinks it. I saw the devil myself when I was seven. He was nothing like McEvoy.'

'Seven,' Fludd said. 'The age of reason. What was he like?'

'A beast. A great rough thing. Breathing outside my bedroom door.'

'You were a brave girl to open it.'

'Oh, I knew I must. I had to see what was there.'

'Did he come another night?'

'He had no need.'

'No. Once is enough.'

'But now,' she said, 'if Father Angwin is right, the devil has come much closer.'

'Indeed. He has taken your arm. He has proffered his assistance. Any time, he seemed to say. At your service. Does that alarm you?'

'The way he rose up just now, out of nowhere it seemed to be . . .'

'I can do that myself,' Fludd said indifferently. 'I have my exits and my entrances. It is cheap. A conjuror's trick.'

'How do I know that it is not you who is the devil?' She came to a halt; they could see the convent below them, and a light burning in an upstairs room. Her voice came out stubborn, hostile. 'A man who pretends to be a priest? Hears confession? Gets people's confidence . . .' And she thought, what if the white flame I felt in my chest was the first flame of that gnawing Hellfire, the fire that renews as it consumes, so that torture is always fresh? What if the unaccountable heat that wrapped me in the shed were from the first blast of Satan's bellows?

'You must choose,' Fludd said, his tone practical. 'I cannot tell you what to think. If you think I am bad for you I will not try to talk you out of it.'

'Bad for me?' She was aghast at his choice of word. Man or devil, she thought, devil or devil's pawn, you'll only damn my immortal soul. That's all you'll do.

'But if I were a devil,' Fludd said, 'I would have a relish for you. It is strange that though you would think the devil a man of fiery tastes, there is nothing he likes better at his banquet than the milk-toast soul of a tender little nun. If I were the devil, you would not be clever enough to find me out. Not until I had dined on you and dined well.'

A long-drawn wail came from Sister Philomena, a wail of shock and distress; then she began to cry. She put her fist in her mouth, and cried around it, her mouth working around the knuckle, bleats escaping from around the bone. In the convent parlour Mother Perpetua waited for her, sitting upright by the dead fire, smiling in the dark.

Chapter Seven

Purpit thumped her. 'Going about like a hoyden,' she said. 'Traipsing through the fields. Out in the night like a tinker.'

She knew it was the fields, and not the roads, because of the burrs and dead leaves that clung to the girl's habit, and because of the mud on her shoes. She did not know the girl had been with Father Fludd. If she did, I would get worse, Philly thought. She's jealous of me, wants him to pay her some attention. No nun, she. Ought to be ashamed. Goes after men. Priests. Tried it with Angwin. Chased her out of the presbytery. Sister Anthony said so. Never forgiven him.

So she kept her own counsel, while Purpit ranted and thumped. This is a sick province, she thought, they're hopeless people. It's a place full of devils, it needs a mission sending to it. It wrestles not against flesh and blood but against principalities, against powers, against the rulers of the darkness of this world. St Paul would have sorted it out.

'Make my convent a laughing stock,' Perpetua said. Thud, thud with her bony knuckles.

Philomena reached out, and grabbed Perpetua's arm, just above the wrist. She held it in her farm-girl's grip. She said nothing, but in her eyes those yellow lights flashed, like chips of gold.

That night, tossing on her hard bed, she couldn't sleep or lie awake; wakefulness seemed the lesser evil. She tried to rouse herself, but marauding nightmares circled her brain like the outriders of a guerrilla band. *Nigredo*, a huge blackamoor, offered her a cigarette from a silver case. *Albedo*, an angel, lit it for her. They wrestled on the allotments, rolling over and over on the rough ground. Later they linked arms, and sang 'Danny Boy'.

At five o'clock she heard the rising bell, and turned over, ramming her face into the pillow. She thought it was a special penitential pillow that Mother Perpetua had decreed for her; it seemed filled with small stones. Sister Anthony was the caller for the week, and she could hear her progress along the corridor, rapping at each door and calling *Dominus vobiscum*.

Philomena yawned, and pushed herself upright in the bed. She fumbled at her throat. The strings of her nightcap were thin and waxy from her sweat. She dug her fingernails into the knot, trying to loosen them. But she hardly had any fingernails. *Dominus vobiscum* fluted outside her door, and Sister Anthony tapped and tapped again. '*Dominus vobiscum*. What are you doing in there, Sister?'

She felt she could not trust her voice. She tilted up her chin, still picking at the knots. If I had scissors, she thought. Scissors of my own. That would be against my vow of holy poverty. If I had a looking-glass. That would be against my vow of holy chastity.

'Goodness gracious me, girl,' Sister Anthony sounded cantankerous now. '*Dominus vobiscum*. Are you deaf?'

The knots unravelled. The cap came off. She dropped it on the coarse blanket. Put her bare feet on the linoleum floor, stretched. Under her shift her upper arms, shoulders, were covered in small blue bruises.

'*Dominus vobiscum*. Are you ill?'

Sick at heart, she thought. '*Et cum spiritu tuo*,' she intoned.

Her voice sounded normal; traitor voice. But her throat ached with tears, and her chest felt clogged with unholy expectation.

'I should think so too,' Sister Anthony said, and passed on.

Later, after an hour on her knees in the chapel, she went into the kitchen and helped Sister Anthony fill the jugs with weak tea, for breakfast.

'I think Father Fludd has the gift of prophecy,' she remarked.

'Is that the case now?' the old nun inquired civilly. 'I wonder will he prophesy something for Aintree.'

'Prophecy doesn't mean telling the future. It means speaking out about the true nature of things.'

Sister Anthony could see that little Philomena had been crying. Dimly she remembered her own early days in the convent, the ritual humiliation and the lonely nights. Since it was she who was in charge of ladling out the breakfast she had it within her means to be kind to the girl; she gave her extra porridge.

Morning: Judd McEvoy, smiling to himself and whistling between his teeth, dusted his shelves and opened up his shop, drawing the bolts on the front door and turning round the cardboard sign that hung in the window. Agnes Dempsey washed up the breakfast dishes. Father Fludd put on his vestments for Mass, praying for each one the correct prayer. Philly could see him, in her mind's eye: amice, alb, cincture, maniple, stole, chasuble. 'Make me white, O Lord, and cleanse my heart . . .'

That morning she had to take a class for a PE lesson. Not her communion class; these children were older. The gloss had gone off them.

First there was dressing them, in the fug of the classroom;

outside it was sharp and cold, and until ten o'clock sparse crystals of frost shone on the ruts of the carriage-drive. The girls, between their desks, had to squirm into thick navy-blue knickers, and out of their frocks and their layers of cardigans; the boys had to take their exercise as best they might in their knee-length grey flannel shorts. There were black pumps to be given out, from the metal cage in the corner of the classroom where they were kept between use: common to the whole class, assorted sizes, in different conditions but mostly poor. Most of the children did not know their shoe size, and if they did they had no way of securing it; there was no method of distribution, merely a free-for-all, and this was the way it had always been. They were enjoined to keep silence during the proceeding; Philomena stood over them, hefty-seeming this morning, her eyes blazing, making sure not a mutter or groan escaped. But the silence of the exercise rendered it no less violent; arms flailed, pinches were delivered, until in some fashion everyone was shod.

Then the procession. Some walked wincingly, their toes mashed together; others, who had made the contrary error, flapped like water birds. In addition – it was mysterious – there were more left pumps than there were right, and Sister Philomena noticed that it was the poorest, the meekest, the most stupid, who were further disadvantaged by this, and had to edge along with their two feet swerving the same way.

The Nissen hut served as a dining room besides a gymnasium, and smelt of dumplings and fat. The trestle-tables and wooden benches were stacked around the room, and on the floor the children set up their equipment. This was what Mother Perpetua called it: the Equipment. 'The Education Committee is sending us Equipment.' Until this year there had only been small oval mats, one per child. They would set them out, and roll about on them; once they began they were no trouble. Then they would stand by the mats, and practise jumping on the spot. It was an exercise suitable for all age groups. Most of them could manage it. And it did not strain their taut nerves.

But the Equipment had added a new terror to their lives. It was shiny and hard, with sharp edges. Just setting it up and fitting it together was a problem for an engineer; the half-clad children sweated beneath its weight, as if they were building bridges for the Japanese. There were steps, and slides. There was a great ladder on supports, that they were meant to swing on, and, she supposed, hoist themselves up and pop their heads between the rungs. And most awful of all, there was a thick round wooden pole; it rested on metal stands, parallel to the ground and at the height of her chest.

'Form teams,' she said, despairingly. 'You, you, you.' None of them wanted to go on the pole. They did not know what to do with it, what to make of it at all. Some, when it came to their turn, crouched beneath and threw their arms around it, and kicked off with their feet, trying to raise themselves and wrap their ankles over its top. It became the vogue, she noticed; each child would attempt it, some with more feebleness than others, few with any lasting success. In the face of the Equipment their timidity became clear, and the extent of their clumsiness, weakness, poor eyesight. They were embarrassed – for it was an emotion that they could feel. They knew that the Equipment had hidden uses, which they could not discern; they knew that other children, some-where else, in happier circumstances, might unlock its secrets. The Equipment was a message that the Education Committee had sent them, to prepare them for the humiliations of their future.

Mass would be long over now, Sister Philomena thought. She stood in a shadow at the side of the hut, letting the children do as they pleased, for she knew that none of the other nuns would come by. Presently they grew tired of their efforts, and fell timidly out of line, eyeing her out of the corners of their eyes, and got out their familiar oval mats;

they bent over, put their skinny grey arms on the floor, and began to do a thing they called bunny-jumps. The two children from Netherhoughton withdrew into a darker corner, and began to hypnotize each other.

He could come and find me, she thought. If he were to inquire at the school they would tell him I was there. But no, he would not do that. He would not inquire.

But he could make some excuse. Something that he wanted me to do for him. What could that be? Now that I am not sacristan, he cannot say, I need polishing doing, Sister, I need extra polishing, I need a very special shine putting on the candlesticks. What could he want then?

But he hardly needs a priest's reasons for what he wants to do, because he is not a priest. Did I know it all along, or just suspect it; did he make a slip, or did I just feel it in my bones? He is just an ordinary man.

But no, she thought, correcting herself. Not that. Not in any sense an ordinary man. What had struck her forcibly, on waking that morning, now occurred to her again; that she had no clear picture of his features in her mind. At Mass, it was true, she had been forced to study him mostly from the back; but had she not been alone with him at the allotments for an hour or more?

Perhaps, she thought, I have looked so intensely that I have been unable to see. I have looked at him as he seems to look at me, with eyes that see beyond the skin. She had heard it said that you could 'devour' someone with your eyes. It was an expression that people used. Yes, that was what she had done. Her eyes had eaten him all up, and rendered his features pulp. Now, like a greedy, heedless child, she had left nothing over for the hour of hunger, the hour of dearth.

When the end of the lesson came, Philomena lined the children up and trailed them along the carriage-drive. The sun had struggled out, and filtered thinly between the bare branches. 'Look, Robin Redbreast.' She pointed to the ditch, where the bird with its mouse-brown back darted in crisp leaves. Yes, Sister, they said dutifully. They looked where she pointed but they did not see. They did not know what they were looking for. Sparrows, they knew; pigeons.

In procession, they rounded the curve of the carriage-drive, and there was Father Fludd: stepping towards them in animated conversation with Agnes Dempsey. Sister Philomena made the children stop, stand aside respectfully while the priest passed. They began, more or less as he drew level, a drawling, yodelling chant. 'Good mo-or-orning Father. Good mo-or-or-ning Miss Dempsey.'

It was the way the children always spoke, when they spoke together. They learnt it at five years old, in the nursery class; learnt it in their first hour at school. Sometimes Philomena thought that if she ever heard it again she would give way to screaming; she would sit on the floor and rend her garments and put ashes on her head, in reparation for the foolishness of the world. Christ died to free us from the burden of our sin, but he never, so far as she could see, lifted a finger to free us from our stupidity.

And as her thoughts ran on, her heart beat faster. She thought it was climbing into her throat, battering there and twisting inside out, contorting in that small space; nobody would see it underneath her habit, but suppose she were some ordinary woman, in a costume and blouse? People would nudge each other; *that poor woman's heart is fighting its way out*. It shocked and amazed her, that the thought should occur – that she should think of herself as a woman, when she was in fact a nun. She felt her face grow red, and her hands begin to tremble. 'Good morning, children,' Fludd said cheerfully. Agnes Dempsey gave them a thin tight smile.

Fludd's eyes flickered over her. He inclined his head, sombre; walked on, his conversation with Miss Dempsey proceeding in lower tones, a more subdued manner. Agnes Dempsey walked more slowly. She took a long look over her shoulder at the young nun; who had turned aside now, and dropped her face, and whose right hand had gone to the wooden crucifix hanging at her chest.

She had not turned aside fast enough to hide her expression from Miss Dempsey – that compound of fear, yearning and excitement, that had yet to be broken down into its elements and recombined by another's will. Agnes, in agitation and sadness, touched her wart. I have missed all my chances in life, she thought. Even a nun has not missed more chances than me. Virgins may see unicorns. Spinsters never do.

This time, when Philomena approached the confessional, she knew it would be Angwin.

She knelt, in the fragrance of polish and tobacco; began at once, rattling her words off. 'Bless me, Father, for I have sinned. It is no time at all since my last confession. I have a question for you. A German friend of mine, who knows only a few words of English . . .'

'Oh, hallo there, my dear,' the priest said.

'. . . was anxious to go to confession, but unfortunately none of the priests in the neighbourhood knew any German. Was my friend obliged to make his confession through an interpreter?'

'Hm,' Father Angwin said. He thought. It was not a problem he had encountered directly, though he had often found the Fetherhoughtonian speech thick and incomprehensible when he had first arrived in the parish. 'Well now,' he said at last, 'do you know what I think he should do? I think he should get one of those dictionaries, a German–English dictionary, and discover what are the names of his sins in English. And as for the number of times he has done each sin, well, he may very quickly learn to count in English, I suppose. Then he might pass a note to the priest in the confessional. Though,' he added, 'it might be as well if the priest were warned as to what were to occur. I should not like to come to hear confessions one day, and find a foreigner poking a paper at me through the grille.'

'So that would be better than an interpreter, would it, Father?'

'I am not ruling out an interpreter, mind. If the need were desperate. Communication is difficult at the best of times, don't you find?' He paused. 'No one should walk around in a state of sin for a moment more than necessary. Perhaps especially not if the person is in a place strange to them. If a person is travelling, you know, there is always a danger of accidents.'

'And if you did use an interpreter, he would be bound by the seal of the confessional, of course.'

'Naturally.' There was another short pause. Angwin said, 'Have you anything to tell me today? Anything about yourself, I mean?'

'No, Father.'

'You are wrestling with your problem still. Your temptation to sin. Or has the temptation passed?'

'No. If anything –'

He cut in. 'I have been praying for you.'

He heard her breathing, beyond the grille and the curtain: the hiccups in her breathing's rhythm, as if she might cry. 'Any more questions today?'

'Oh yes, many.'

She reads them off a paper, he thought.

'A doctor has human bones in his possession, from the days of his studies. He is anxious to get rid of them. He got them while he was a student in a Protestant country.'

'Germany again?'

She stopped. His question had thrown her. He was not meant to interrupt. 'Do go on.'

'Where is he supposed to bury them?'

'Protestant bones,' Father said. 'I hardly know.'

'In Ireland,' she said timidly, 'there are special plots, in the major hospitals, for burying the bits of bodies that are taken away in operations.'

'There may be a similar dispensation here.'

'If they might be useful to some hospital, he could donate them?'

She has answers on her paper, he thought, as well as questions. 'I don't see why not.'

'But he must be reverent with them, must he not? They were part of a living body once, he must recollect, and that body was the temple of the spirit. Even though it was a Protestant. Probably.'

'Again,' Father Angwin said, 'if in the parish there were a funeral, I mean just in the ordinary course of events, a funeral of some elderly person . . . and the relatives could be prevailed upon . . . it might be a good thing to lay them to rest in that way.'

'Protestant bones in a Catholic grave . . .' She paused for thought. 'Just say nothing to the relatives,' she said. 'That would be my way. Because you know how people are. They wouldn't take account of how old the bones were, they'd carry on about it just the same. Just slip them in, while the mourners are all gossiping. That would be how to do it. There's no need to cause unnecessary fuss and alarm, and give people a chance to get on their high horses.'

'Do I know this doctor?'

'Oh no, Father.'

'Because I was thinking . . . I myself have this graveyard. Of sorts.' But I am like the elder Tobias, he thought: 'wearied with burying'.

She said, 'It is a hypothetical case.'

'Yes. Of course it is. Any more?'

He felt that she moved closer; that she had shuffled forward on her kneeler, and put her face inches from his own.

'Suppose I can save a man from drowning. And I have not

the courage to do it? Am I in justice bound to repair the loss to his family?'

'Repair the loss? Well, how could you do that?'

'I was considering their situation in life. How they would be left. Financially. They would be badly off. He would be the breadwinner. And suppose I could have saved him – should I make some restitution, do you think? Am I obliged to?'

'In justice, no. In charity, perhaps.'

This is the world we inhabit, he thought: burning houses, drowning men, alien bones on the loose; all perplexity and pain to the tender conscience, that cannot speak of its dearest concerns.

'I think that is enough,' he said, 'in the way of hypotheses.'

'If you think . . .' she said, 'if you think of a sin, but you do not do it, can that be as bad as if you had actually done it?'

'It can be. I would need to know more.'

'Supposing a person entertains certain thoughts . . . but he does not know at the time that they are bad? Suppose they start off as quite ordinary, permissible thoughts, but then he feels where they are tending?'

'He should stop thinking at once.'

'But you cannot stop thinking. Can you? Can you?'

'A good Catholic can.'

'How?'

'Prayer.'

'Prayer drives thought out?'

'With practice.'

'I don't know,' she said. 'It has been my experience that you can pray but the thoughts run under the prayers, like wires under the ground.'

'Then you are not doing it properly.'

'I have tried.'

'Trying is not enough.' He almost spoke out, giving their game away. He almost said, remember what you were taught in your novitiate. It is not enough to do a thing as well as you can. You must do it perfectly.

'It is impossible, isn't it?' she said. 'You begin innocent enough, but you can't walk around with your eyes shut, with your ears shut, with your mind a blank. But once you see and hear and think . . . things lead to things.'

'Oh yes,' he said. 'They do that.'

When his penitent had left, Father Angwin gave her time to get out of the church; then, out of old habit, he crossed himself, though he did not see any point in it, and did not believe in the cross, and did not believe he was redeemed; and silently rose, and left the confessional. There, whisking around the corner into the porch, was Dempsey's pleated skirt.

'Agnes,' he called, his voice surprisingly, sacrilegiously loud. 'What are you doing there?'

Miss Dempsey froze to the spot, her fingers in the holy-water stoup. He strode down the centre aisle and bore down on her.

'Saying my prayers, Father.' Her voice was placid; her face told a different story.

'I see. You are unwontedly pious, for the middle of the day. What are you praying for? Have you a special intention?'

Oh yes, she thought. That there should be a splendid scandal in the parish – for we need a good shake-up. 'I have been praying for the suppression of heresy, the exaltation of the Church and concord amongst Christian princes,' she replied.

Since her Child of Mary's handbook obliged her to do this, and regularly, there was nothing Father Angwin could say.

That evening it turned colder. A wind soughed across the

moors, out of England's autumnal heart; a wind with no breath of the sea, bearing an upland odour of privation and loss. Darkness came early, seeming to swell from the high ground above the church and roll down the carriage-drive, a carpet of night that pushed the children before it, down Church Street and into their lighted homes in Chapel Street and Back Lane. When the last of them had left the gates, the nuns locked the school doors with iron keys, and hurried in concert back to their refectory, to the tea and bread and margarine that Sister Anthony had prepared for them.

The margarine had a peculiar, sharp taste tonight, as if something had got mixed with it – which was perfectly possible, as Sister Anthony was absent-minded now, and short-sighted, and, some believed, malicious. The meal was eaten in the silence enjoined by the Rule; but there would be plenty said about the marge, at a later date. The faces of Polycarp, Ignatius Loyola and Cyril were twisted with the effort they made to hold back scathing speech. Their complaints rolled about their mouths, like loose teeth.

The next collation would be the last of the day, and it would be soup. Philomena imagined she could smell it already. She pictured herself, in her place at table; for places never changed, unless someone came or went – or died, which would be more likely. Soon I shall be sitting here again, she thought, after the evening routine: after the hard kneeler in the convent chapel, directly behind Sister Cyril: after the Sorrowful Mysteries of the Rosary, and sundry other prayers. The nightly Examination of Conscience, the sign of the cross, then the kitchen, to help Sister Anthony serve, and collect my share of black looks and blame. Into the big blue apron, and out with the tureen and the ladle; the usual draught rattles the windows as I step down the corridor to the refectory carrying the tureen, elbows jutting out. 'Bless us, oh Lord, and these thy gifts . . .' The small clank of the metal ladle on the side of each bowl. Spoon raised to lips; she tasted the soup, a greyish, frothy liquid, oversalted, scraps of vegetables (or perhaps peelings) awash in its depths.

A violent pain in her ribs made her jump back, almost drop off the refectory bench. She stifled her exclamation; why add another fault to the fault that Perpetua had just discerned? It was that rigid, cruel forefinger again, meant to wipe the expression off her face; she knew it must have been there, that blank dreaming expression that Purpit took as a personal affront. Her brief absence of mind had put away the day as if she were folding it into a box, telescoped all the time between the bread-and-margarine collation and the soup collation.

But what did it matter? Certainly, when time passed in the ordinary world at its ordinary rate, it would bring her to the same seat, the same spoon, the same sensation, the same salt-and-sour taste on her tongue. All her life was reducible perhaps to one long day, starting with the caller's *Dominus vobiscum* and ending with private prayer before the crucifix in her cell, knees chilled by the linoleum. If every day from now on was to be the same, why have the days at all, why not elide them somehow and live the next forty years in a minute? She lowered her head, as if examining the grain in the wood of the refectory table. I have reached, she thought, a human being's lowest ebb; I have no curiosity about the future. I know what the future will be; the Rule sets it out for me. She looked up at Perpetua, her present vision blurred, her eyes dwelling still on what was to come, and for the first time, a thought occurred to her: whoever regulates my future steals it from me.

And if the future is predictable, does that mean it is planned? If it is predictable, is it in the least controllable? This is old stuff, she thought, in disgust with herself: this is seminarians' stuff. Is my will free? Outside the wind dropped. The nuns, draining the dregs of their tea, lifted their heads and looked at each other across the table. It was as if in the sudden silence they discerned a voice, a voice speaking out of turn. It was a moment of expectancy, unease. A curious ripple ran around the table. Overhead, the forty-watt bulb that the Order approved flickered once, twice, three times: like St Peter's denials of Christ. Then gaunt shadows turned their faces down, and muttered a grace; then rose, as if in the grip of flames, and flickered from the room.

The priests had eaten early: hotpot. At least, Father Angwin had eaten his, he did not know what Fludd might have done. It was the usual tale: a full plate, then an empty plate, and that discreet mastication in between quite insufficient to account for the disappearance of the curate's supper.

Then, too, Father Angwin was seriously concerned about the level of the whisky in his bottle. However much he drank nowadays, it never seemed to drop. Many the night he had said to the curate, we'll be needing a new bottle if we are to have a drink together tomorrow; but then he had contrived, in the course of the day, to dismiss the unpleasant fact from his mind. And in the evening there always seemed to be enough. Not enough to hold a party with, mind. Not a quantity of whisky. But a sufficiency.

'This place has gone very quiet,' Father Angwin said, helping the curate to a glass.

'The wind has dropped.'

'No, I mean in general. It's since you came. You haven't maybe without telling me done a spot of exorcism?'

'No,' Fludd said. 'But I have been up and done a spot of minor repair work on the guttering. I take an interest in such matters. I was able to borrow a ladder from a pious household in Netherhoughton. And I have consulted with Judd McEvoy about the downspouts. For a tobacconist, he is very well-informed. He fears the church too needs quite extensive structural renovations. But he says it would cost a mint of money.'

'It wasn't the drips and creaks that bothered us, though,' Father Angwin said. 'We were accustomed to those. But we used to get feet walking up and down overhead, and various banging noises, and you would feel that someone had come in. Or the door would be kicked open, and no one would enter.'

'Well, I entered,' Fludd said. 'Did I not? Eventually.'

'Agnes was of the opinion that the house was full of discarnate entities.'

'Of a malign sort?'

'We hardly knew. But Agnes believes in a multiplicity of devils. In that, she is of quite an old-fashioned turn of mind.'

'Yes, I understand you. There is this lax modern way of talking about "the devil". It surprises me. When you consider that for centuries some of the finest minds in Europe were occupied in counting devils and finding out their various characters.'

'Reginald Scot, I think, towards the end of the sixteenth century, made it fourteen million. Give or take.'

'I can be more precise,' Fludd said. 'He made it fourteen million, one hundred and ninety-eight thousand, five hundred and eighty. That excluded, of course, the lords and princes of Hell. That was just the ordinary drone devils.'

'But in those days,' Father Angwin said, 'if a devil put in an appearance, they had spells for binding him and questioning him and getting his name and number out of him. They understood very well that devils had their specialities, and that each devil was quite distinct in personality.'

'St Hilary tells us that each devil had his particular bad smell.'

'But now people just say "Satan", or "Lucifer". It is the curse of the present century, this rage for oversimplification.'

'Sister Philomena told me,' Fludd said, sipping his whisky, 'that she had encountered a devil as a child. She said that he was nothing like Judd McEvoy. But then, why should he be?'

Father Angwin looked away. 'I know that no one agrees with me, in the matter of Judd. But you see, Father Fludd, we do not have the privileges of a former age. Devils do not so readily manifest themselves. Not within the range of our vision. Sister Philomena has been singularly fortunate. When she thinks of a devil she can put a face to it.'

'You have tried to do the same.'

'Every devil must have a face. Even if it is a wolf's face, even if it is a serpent's face, even if it is a tobacconist's. It must be something we can know and recognize, it must be in our own image or very close to it, it must be animal or human or some hybrid of the two. Because what else can we imagine? What else have we seen?'

'Demonology,' Fludd said, taking a sip. 'It is an unbearable subject. Deep and unbearable. Especially for you, Father. Since you ceased to believe in God.'

'If it had not been for McEvoy,' Angwin said, looking away again, 'I don't know whether the notion of the devil would have such a strong grip on me either. My mind might have taken a secular turn. I might have become some kind of rational man.'

'I have seen changes.' Fludd followed the other man's gaze, and looked into the fire. 'There was a time when the air was packed with spirits, like flies on an August day. Now I find that the air is empty. There is only man and his concerns.'

Father Angwin sat hunched and brooding, his whisky glass between the palms of his hands. The bottle was as full as ever. 'I am ill,' he said. 'My soul chooseth hanging, and my bones death.'

'My dear fellow,' said Fludd, removing his gaze from the fire, and fastening it anxiously on the priest's face.

'Oh, a quotation,' Angwin said. 'A biblical quotation. The Old Testament, you know. Book of somebody-or-other.'

Fludd thought of Sister Philomena, striding over the fields, failing to recognize his own quotations. When he thought of the nun, a soft, creeping uneasiness made itself felt; it was located in his solar plexus. Well now, he said to himself. I never knew that I had human feelings. He reached for his glass.

'I am like Father Surin,' Angwin said.

'Forgive me. I never knew him.'

'I mean the exorcist of Loudun.' Father rose, levering himself up with his hands on the arms of his chair; Fludd had noticed how, in the short time he had been in the parish, the priest's movements had slowed, and his animated features had become masked by a frozen disappointment and grief. He had carried on his pretence so well, so long, never by word or deed betraying the disillusion at the core of his priestly vocation. But my coming here has changed things, Fludd thought; falseness can no longer be endured, truth must out. There must be new combinations within the heart: passions never witnessed, notions never before formed. 'What was I saying?' Angwin asked. 'Ah yes, Father Surin.' He went to the bookcase, took out a volume, opened it at a place he had marked. '*When I wish to speak my speech is cut off; at Mass I am brought up short; at confession I suddenly forget my sins; and I feel the devil come and go within me as if he were at home*. I translate,' he said, 'freely.' He closed the book and put it back on the shelf. 'Father Surin lost all consciousness of God. He entered on a state of melancholy. His illness lasted for twenty years. In the end he could not read or write, he could not walk and he had to be carried everywhere. He had not the strength to lift his arms to change his shirt. His attendants beat him. He grew old and paralysed and mad.'

'But he was cured, was he not? In the end.'

'What cures melancholy, Father Fludd?'

Fludd said, 'Action.'

*

At midnight, Fludd went out alone. It was cold, clear, still; a dried-up half-moon was skewered against the sky. The upper air was full of snow, the year's first. He could hear his own footsteps. He let his torch-beam loose among the trees, then brought it back to his side, as if it were a serpent he were training.

The old wooden doors of the garage were quite rotten. They should have been painted, he thought, with some kind of wood preservative, if they were to withstand the Fetherhoughton weather. There was a key somewhere, but he had not wanted to advertise his intentions by asking for it. He stood back and gave the door a good kick.

Sister Philomena sat up in bed – quite suddenly, as if she had been given an electrical shock – and her hair – what there was of it – rose on the back of her neck. She threw back the covers, put her feet on the chilly floor. When she stood up a pain darted through her joints, as if her bones were filed sharp.

I am a wreck, she thought. Her ribs and shoulders still ached from Purpit's recent assaults. She went to the small attic window, and peered out. Not an owl: no nightbird, no storm, no lightning flash. She did not know what had woken her. Her window was at the back of the convent; beyond lay the slumbering moors, unseen but always present, like the life of the mind. The thought of the moors made her shudder. What anarchy in heaven the day those moors were made. *Anything may happen*, she thought. Her nape prickled again. She stared at the black treetops: but not for long.

Miss Dempsey fumbled, and found: her candlewick bedspread, her knees, and her dressing-gown, draped decorously over the end of her bed. She pulled it towards her and, still sitting up in bed, wriggled her arms into it and fastened it across her chest. The room seemed more than usually cold.

The brass-belled alarum clock said ten past twelve. Are they still down there, carousing, she thought? Is that what woke me, Father falling over?

If he has fallen over, she thought, he will need another cup of cocoa, and strong admonition. That young little devil doesn't seem to have a need of sleep, or else he sleeps so sound in the few hours he takes that it does him more good than it does the rest of us.

Miss Dempsey eased her feet into her bedroom slippers. They were the standard Fetherhoughton sort, with a nylon-fur ruff of powder blue. They made no sound as she passed along the corridor, and set them on the stairs.

At the foot of the stairs, she stopped and listened. But there was nothing to hear: not the expected murmur of voices, nor the snoring of Father Angwin fallen asleep in his chair. She sensed at once that she was alone in the house, and this sensation was enough to send her, despite the cold and her state of undress, hurtling out of the front door and into the night.

A dry leaf touched his cheek. Father Angwin stood quivering, a fox at bay. Waking suddenly, he had scrambled from his bed and had pulled on his clothes, armed himself with the presbytery's other torch, and taken the stairs two at a time, impelled by he hardly knew what; and I said I was paralysed, he thought, I told Fludd that soon I would need people to carry me about. He heard the dull grate of metal striking stone; then nothing more, but a soft sound of funerals, earth falling on earth with its familiar hiss.

Yet not the sound of funerals, but anti-funerals. He approached the broken ground, the private graveyard that he had mentioned to Philly in the confessional, which he had offered for the use of her Protestant bones.

Fludd, he saw. Elegant back bent. Digging. Digging like an Irishman. And as he watched, the curate stepped back, and with a cavalier gesture, holding his spade at chest height, tossed the soil and gravel over his left shoulder.

'Holy God,' Father Angwin said. He approached the excavation, his black feet sliding on the frosty ground. He flashed his torch-beam into the hole. 'Would we have such a thing as a second shovel?'

Chapter Eight

Torches were not enough; and when they had debated what to do, Father Angwin took from his pocket the key of the sacristy, and handed it to Philomena. 'But I am not sacristan any more,' she said. 'Purpit took it away from me.'

'Tonight is not an ordinary night. These are extraordinary circumstances. Agnes, go with her. Open the top cupboard, on the left. You'll find half a dozen old candlesticks. Bring some of the big tall High Mass candles, you know where they are. We'll plant them around the place.'

'I have household candles,' Agnes said.

'Don't waste time,' Father said. 'Off you go.'

In the church porch, Philly gave Miss Dempsey her hand, feeling that she should somehow be the stronger of the two. The door into the church opened with its customary groan, like a jaded actor falling back on proven effects; and they made their way together up the centre aisle, over the familiar stone flags, mouths open slightly, swallowing in the darkness. There was a moment when Miss Dempsey disappeared; Philly's stomach squeezed tight in sudden terror, and she clutched at the empty air. But the housekeeper was only genuflecting; she bobbed up again, with a whispered apology, and they moved closer together and tiptoed on.

In the sacristy they spoke, short and to the point; Philly got up on a chest, and unlocked the cupboard, and found what Father wanted. She handed down the candlesticks, one by one, and Agnes grappled them to her bosom, and jiggled them to herself with an upraised knee. Philly jumped down, and chose six candles from the box, running her fingertips over the arches of creamy wax.

When they returned, Father Fludd was leaning on his spade; Father Angwin, like a sprite, sat cross-legged on the ground. He jumped up, '*Fiat lux*. Delve away, my boy.'

Philomena knelt on the ground by the hole Father Fludd had made, and put out one finger, experimentally, as if the earth were water and she were going to bath a baby. Below the loose surface the soil felt heavy, saturated. She felt something move, against her finger: as it might be, a worm. 'Oh,' she said, pulling her hand away: the refinements of the convent parlour. 'Worm,' she said.

'Don't frighten me,' Father Angwin said.

Fludd said, 'We see devils in serpents. We see serpents in worms. They are things within our common experience.'

Philomena glanced up. She imagined a sceptical glittering expression in his eyes, although really it was too dark to see any expression at all. Agnes Dempsey said, 'As for worms, we all know where they are coming from and going to.'

There was a silence. They looked down at the graves. Candle flames flickered in the air, doubling and bowing like genii let out of bottles; their eyes grew accustomed to such light as there was, and they wished that they had not, for the priest, the nun and the housekeeper were able to see in each other's faces a reflection of their own unease.

When Philly explored again, she found something solid, thin, hard and sharp. 'It's O K, you've done it, Father Fludd,' she said. 'We're down to them. They weren't too deep at all.'

Without speaking, Father Angwin dropped to his knees beside her. She saw his breath, a smoky plume in the air. The snow above was too hard and cold to fall; if you could shake heaven tonight, it would rattle like a cradle toy. The priest leant forward, one hand steadying himself, the other groping in the shallow pit. 'I feel it,' he said. 'Father Fludd, I feel it. Agnes, I feel it. I think it is the edge of St Cecilia's portable organ.'

'Let me scrape with my spade,' said Fludd.

'No, no. You might damage it.' Father Angwin crouched, both hands dabbling and patting at what lay beneath the soil.

'If we are not to use the spade,' Agnes said, 'the excavations will not be done by dawn.'

'Miss Dempsey, you are ill-protected against the elements,' Fludd said, 'I did not notice, when you so suddenly arrived. Should you not go back indoors and dress more sensibly?'

'Thank you, Father,' Agnes said. She blushed red under cover of the night. 'I have this warmish flannelette nightgown on underneath.' She shivered; but she could not tear herself away.

Philomena at least was properly dressed. When she had turned from the window of her room, excitement and fear had guttered inside her, a blaze about to start; but she must roll on those thick woollen stockings, pull on her drawers. Her heart pounding, she must shake out the three petticoats the Order prescribed, and lash them about her waist, knotting their sashes and strings. She must punch her arms through her stout scratchy bodice, her cheeks growing hot, and fumble with her shaking fingers at the buttons at its neck. What a time it took, what an agonizing time, what an eternity to climb into her habit, the black folds stifling and gagging her. Then her undercap with its drawstrings, and the tiny safety-pins to secure it, and all the time the knowledge of the necessary encounter, waiting out there in the frozen night. Fludd is adjacent, he is proximate, he is nigh; and here she juggles with her starched white outer cap, ramming it on to her skull, pressing it over the brows, feeling it bite into its accustomed sore groove on her forehead; and now she scrab bles for the long straight pins to secure her veil, and now she drops one, and hears them – yes, in the midnight silence of the convent, hears a pin drop, and roll. So now she must throw herself to her knees and pad with her hands and dab the floor under the bed, and then, rising successful, pin pinched between her fingers, catch the back of her head a glancing blow on the under-edge of the bedstead; iron on bone. Sick, half-stunned, emerging from under the bedstead on hands and knees, she must lever herself up and put on her veil, skewering it with the pins, and then seize up her crucifix and drop it over her head, then lay hold of the long swinging string of her rosary beads and whip it out into the room and secure it around her waist. Then – the breath of the future misting the panes, the future grinning at the window eager to have her in its jaws – she must bend again, dizzily, pick up her shoes, pluck at the knots in the laces which, contrary to holy obedience and all the dictates of the Order, she has left fastened the night before. Then, gasping with irritation, she must fling the shoes to the floor, work her feet into them still fastened, stamp and then jump them into place; thrust her handkerchief into her pocket, and then, only then, cross herself, murmur a short prayer for guidance, open the door of her cell, make her way along the passage, down the stairs and swerve sharp right, ignoring the big front door, and through the passage to the empty, echoing kitchen. She had not dared to put on a light, but the moon from a clear sky shone through the kitchen window, a small, mean, wintry moon, palely gilding the ladle and the tureen, the up-ended pans on their rack, the jugs standing ready for morning tea. She had tugged at the bolts of the back door, and held her breath as she drew them back; then she had pulled the door shut behind her, and run out into the night.

Now Miss Dempsey leant forward, and put a hand on Philomena's shoulder to steady herself. Grunting with effort, the housekeeper got to her knees; sucking her underlip, she put out her hands to feel the ground. 'I beg to differ, Father Angwin. I don't think it is the portable organ. I think it is the edge of St Gregory's Papal tiara.'

'Let me at it,' said Fludd. 'I won't smash a thing.'

'You are both wrong,' Philomena said. 'What you can feel there has no thickness at all. It is the arrow that pierces the heart of St Augustine.'

'We had better yield to Father Fludd,' the priest said. 'Two women and an ageing fellow like me, what can we do against superior strength? Go at it, my dear.'

'Move aside, Sister,' Fludd said. Unwilling to stand up and retreat, she remained on her knees and shuffled two feet to the left. His braced knee brushed her upper arm. He aligned the tip of his spade, and then she heard the sickening squelch and clatter: steel on plaster. He had driven it in, right by (she believed) St Agatha's head; as if the virgin were to be martyred again.

'Careful, careful,' said Agnes, clasping her hands; Father Angwin breathed, 'Steady on.' But Philly moved forward on to hands and knees, her eyes on the edge of the spade; she wanted to be the first to see, the first to catch a glimpse of the face emerging from its grave.

Father Fludd planted his foot in the trench he had made; it was an inch, perhaps, to the left of Agatha's shoulder. He seemed not to feel her own urgency to uncover one particular set of features; his efforts were general, unspecific. But then, she thought, he did not know the statues, not as individuals. His curiosity did not focus on one or the other. Long before he came to the parish, they had been buried.

'St Jerome,' she whispered up at him. She pointed. 'Over there. Uncover the lion.'

'You should get up,' he said, pausing for a moment, but not looking directly at her. 'You'll take a chill.'

'Agnes,' Father Angwin said, 'would it not be the best service you could render if you brought us cocoa?'

Fludd's spade scraped away; the tip of a nose appeared, startlingly white.

'Oh, I could not,' Miss Dempsey said. 'Forgive me, Father. I could not leave now.'

Philomena launched herself forward once again. With her fingers she scooped the earth away. It was Agatha, indeed. Philly pinched out the plaster cheekbones. She passed a finger over the sealed lips. Then, flinching, over the painted retina.

'Shine your torch, Father Angwin,' she said. She wanted to see the face; and as soon as she did so, she knew that this interval, this suspension, this burial had brought about a change. She did not mention this change to the others; she realized that it might be something only she could see. But the virgin's expression had altered. Blankly sweet, she had become sly; unyielding virtue had yielded; she gazed up, with a conspiratorial smile, into Heaven's icy vault.

Soon they ceased to speak; the cold crept into their bones. They heard one o'clock strike. Bulky outlines were seen, still shrouded by the soil. Then parts of saints emerged; an elbow, a foot, St Apollonia's pincers. In silence they recognized and greeted each one. When St Jerome and the lion came out, Sister Philomena jumped into the trench, and Fludd paused, leaning on the spade, allowing her to clear the beast's features with her hands. Her feet slipped, as she regained her place with the others; Father Angwin put out a hand to steady her, and she clung to him for a moment, leaning heavily on his arm, as if she were winded.

Then Fludd stopped digging, and said 'Listen. Somebody's coming.'

'Who goes there?' called Miss Dempsey: introducing a military note. But without reply or preamble, the new arrival was upon them, transfixed for a moment like a rabbit in the beam of Father Angwin's torch, yet wearing an expression too smug, too imperturbable, for a rabbit to wear. Then he shone his own flashlight, right into the priest's eyes.

'It is I. Judd McEvoy.'

'Good morning, Judd,' Father Angwin said. 'Why are you out at this hour? If I may inquire?'

'I have been down to Fetherhoughton,' Judd replied. 'I wanted a basin of peas.'

'So that is what you have there.'

'Yes, and fish. In my newspaper.'

'I did not know the shop was still open at this hour.'

'They fry very late, these nights, to oblige anyone from up the hill who might feel peckish. We people up the hill are never early to bed. When the nights are long, we take advantage of them.'

'Not you surely, Judd.' Father Angwin faced him across the graves. 'Surely you, a pillar of the Men's Fellowship, you don't go in for their rites?'

'Oh, I am aware that you have your opinion of me, Father.' Judd's tone was airy. 'You speak as if you mean to shame me into some admission. But when I say "we", I speak of my neighbours. I speak of the Netherhoughtonians. It was an expression, merely an expression. Would you like some of my fish?'

'Be careful there,' Father Angwin said. 'You have almost got your foot on Ambrose.'

Judd looked down. 'So I have.' With a delicacy and sureness that suggested to Father Angwin that he was indeed of nocturnal habit, the tobacconist picked his way through the trenches. 'It is a pity I did not come on the scene earlier. By way of the footpaths it is no distance to my home. I could have brought my own spade. Father Fludd has had everything to do.'

'Why have you a spade, Judd? You have no garden.'

'You forget, Father, that I was one of the allotment holders. In the old days.'

'Were you so? Then why could you not influence your brutish compatriots? Could you not turn away the raiding parties from their careers of crime and violence?'

'Oh, I am not a man who would turn a person away from anything,' Judd said. 'Or towards anything, either. I am by nature merely an onlooker. This enterprise of yours, for example, this secret and private enterprise – I regard it with complete equanimity. You have not asked my opinion, I have not given it. Nothing would induce me to give it. I am one of the world's bystanders.'

I knew you were a devil, Father Angwin thought. Bystanders are an evil breed.

'They do say,' Agnes put in timidly, 'that the onlooker sees most of the game.'

'Quite so,' Judd said. 'Miss Dempsey, I am sure you will not refuse a piece of my fish?' He unwrapped his newspaper. A delicious aroma crept out.

'Well, I am tempted,' Miss Dempsey said.

'Sister Philomena,' Judd said, enticingly. 'Now, there is so little here that I am sure you could not offend the canons of your Order.'

'I'm starving,' Philly said.

McEvoy proffered the parcel. Father Angwin broke off a piece of fish. Soon they all ate, Father Fludd picking at a flake or two. It was cold but good. 'I wonder,' Father Angwin said, 'whether it was fried in lard, or dripping?' He looked at Philomena inquiringly. But she would not meet his eye. His spirits rose; he felt quite jocular, feasting like this in the presence of his enemy, and on his enemy's own supper. 'I wish we might have a fish each,' he said; looking inquiringly again, but this time at Father Fludd. He wondered whether the curate might effect some sort of multiplication. After all, there was a precedent for it. But Fludd, though his portion had been smaller than any, continued to eat.

*

'It seems to me now,' Fludd said, 'that we should wait for full daylight. We need ropes, and brute strength.'

'The Children of Mary,' Miss Dempsey said at once. 'It is our meeting tomorrow.'

'Tonight, you mean,' Philly said.

'We would undertake to wash them down. I believe the president would allow it. We could do our litany and so on at the same time.'

'I cannot think why you ever agreed to bury them,' Fludd said.

'You don't know the bishop.' Philomena brushed earth from her habit. 'If we'd have left them exposed, he might have come up here with a mallet and smashed them all to bits.'

'I think your imagination is running away with you, Sister,' Agnes said. 'And of course Father Fludd knows the bishop.'

'We still have the bishop to contend with,' Angwin said. 'Our sudden bravado does not make him vanish away.'

'He could ban the statues all over again,' Miss Dempsey said. 'Our night's work could be wasted.'

'Not wasted,' Judd said. 'At least you have not been bystanders. Father Angwin will value that in you.'

Agnes touched the priest's arm. 'What if he tells us to get rid of them all over again? Will we defy him?'

'You could have a schism,' Father Fludd said.

'I thought of it before.' Father Angwin also brushed earth from himself. 'But I lacked heart.'

'You say "you", Father Fludd,' observed McEvoy. 'You do not say "we". May I take it that you will not be amongst us for very long?'

Fludd did not answer. He put his spade over his shoulder. 'I have done all I am going to do,' he said. 'Miss Dempsey, I think you should make a warming drink. Perhaps you could light the oven and warm Mr McEvoy's peas for him. He has been kept from their enjoyment.'

Faces looked up from the ground; bone-coloured, blank-eyed, staring at the snow-charged sky. Miss Dempsey gathered her dressing-gown more closely about her. Wordlessly, she put her arm through Father Angwin's, and they turned towards the presbytery. The priest shone his torch before them to pick out the path. The tobacconist followed.

'I must go back,' Philly whispered. The clock struck. 'We get up at five.'

'That was half-past two. I do not suppose they are in bed in Netherhoughton.' Fludd put out his hand. She hesitated for a moment, then placed hers in it.

'There's plenty of tonight left,' Fludd said.

They turned downhill, towards the convent. Before them the hard ground gleamed silver with frost. Behind them the abandoned candles flickered. Around them was an argentine brightness, solar and lunar, unearthly and mercurial, sparkling from the dead branches, flickering in the ditch, glinting on the cobbles before the church door. The convent windows were washed with brightness, the grimy stonework glowed; high on the terraces, fireflies seemed to dart.

All my life till now, she thought, has been a journey in the dark. But now another kind of travelling begins: a long vagrancy under the sun, in its sacred and vivifying light.

When three o'clock struck, Fludd placed on her forehead – just below the place where the white band bit into it – a chaste, dry kiss. A sacramental kiss, she thought. At the thought, she closed her eyes. Fludd bent his head. She felt the tip of his tongue flick across her eyelids. 'Philly,' he said, 'you know, don't you, what you have to do?'

'Yes, I know I have to get out.'

'You know that you must do it soon.'

'It will take years,' she said. 'My sister, they just threw her out on her ear. But she was a novice. I'm professed. It'll have to go to the bishop. It'll have to go to Rome.'

Fludd left her for a moment, moved away. As soon as his body ceased to touch hers, she felt the creeping cold, and felt her courage ebb. There was no moon now; only a single Mass candle, placed where she had left it, lit again with Fludd's cigarette lighter. And there were the pans, up-ended on their rack, the pans that she had so often scrubbed for Sister Anthony; and there were the tea jugs, waiting for the morning.

Fludd walked about the kitchen. His feet made no sound on the stone floor. She craved real sunlight, a July day; to see him clearly, know what he looked like.

'You don't have to go to Rome.'

'I wish it were summer,' she whispered.

'Did you hear what I said? You don't have to go to Rome.'

'But I do. I have to be dispensed from my vows. There are papers to be forwarded. Only the Vatican can do it.'

Summer will come, she thought. And I will be here still, waiting; for who will expedite the matter, I have no friends. And another winter will come, and a summer, and another winter. By that time, where will he be?

'You're not taking in what I say,' Fludd told her. 'You say you have to be dispensed, I say you don't have to be dispensed. You say you are bound, I say you are not bound. What law do you think keeps you here?'

'The law of the Church,' she said, startled. 'Oh, no, I suppose that's not a law. Not like the law of the land. But Father Fludd –'

'Don't call me that,' he said. 'You know the truth of the matter.'

'– but Father Fludd, I would be excommunicated.'

Fludd moved towards her again. The candle flared upward, as if the flame had breathed. He touched her face, the back of her neck; began to draw the pins out of her veil.

She jumped back. 'You mustn't,' she said. 'Oh no. No, you mustn't.'

He desisted for a moment. Fell back. His expression was dubious. He did not seem tired. His stamina was wonderful. Philomena turned her head suddenly, attracted by a movement at the window. The snow had begun to fall; big flakes, fleecy, brushing the glass without a sound. She watched it. 'It must be warmer outside. It'll never stick, will it? It won't last the night.'

For she knew that nothing as good as that could ever happen for her; God would not arrange it that when she jerked at five o'clock from her edgy doze she would creep to the window and see a new landscape, its features obliterated, its ground untrodden, its black trees hung with bridal veils. No: the snow would be the night's hallucination, a phantasm of the small hours. Tomorrow at five there would be no sun or snow, she would look from the window and see nothing but her own face dimly reflected in the pane; but if dawn by some freak of nature broke so early, it would reveal only the dark, swollen edge of the moors, and the web of branches near at hand, and a section of the drain-spout, and the sparrows hopping along the guttering in search of food. She would see the same old world; the one in which she had to live. I can't bear it, she thought; not one more day. Her hands crept to her throat; then to her temples and the cloth of her veil; then to the nape of her neck; then searched out the pins.

Fludd took the pins from her one by one, and laid them in a line on the edge of the kitchen table. He set his long fingers on either side of her head and lifted off the vice of her white cap. She had only the strength she needed to make her decision, to give in to him; she felt weak now, limp and cold and beyond resisting anything. He took out the safety-pins from her linen inner cap, and set them on the table beside the straight pins. With one neat firm pull, he freed the drawstring, and lifted off her cap, and dropped it on the floor.

'You look like a badly cut hedge,' he said.

She felt a blush creep over her exposed neck. 'Sister Anthony does it. Once a month. Everybody. Even Purpit. The scissors are rusty. We don't have our own. I've often wished for a pair. It's against holy poverty.'

Fludd ran his hand over her head. The hair, an inch long in places, grew this way and that; here was a neglected tendril growing into curl, here was a bald patch, here was a bristly tuft fighting its way upward like a spring shoot fighting for light and air. 'What was it like?' he said.

'Brown. Quite ordinary brown. It had a bit of a wave.'

It seemed to him, as far as he could judge in the poor light, that the proportions of her face were altered now. It was smaller and softer; her eyes were less watchfully large, and her lips had lost their pinched nun-look. She seemed to have melted away, and remoulded herself into some other woman whom he had never met. He kissed her on the mouth; less sacramentally now.

At nine o'clock McEvoy came to the back door with a wheelbarrow. Agnes jumped out of her skin when she heard his knock. She wiped the washing-up suds from her hands, and hurried to the door.

'Mr McEvoy. Who is minding your shop?'

The tobacconist removed his checked cap respectfully. 'A dear friend,' he said.

'Have you got ropes there too?'

'I have everything requisite. I think the barrow is the way to manage.'

'I suppose you have told everybody?'

'Nothing of the night's events has passed my lips. The parish will know soon enough.'

'The Children of Mary will know tonight.'

'The nuns will know earlier, no doubt. If Father Fludd is willing and able, we can have all the saints back on their plinths in an hour or two.' He smiled faintly. 'When we

buried them, there was quite a crowd to help us. Digging
things up is not so hard as digging them in, is it?'

It was harder for me, Miss Dempsey thought. 'I will call
Father Fludd,' she said. 'He was up as usual to say Mass. He
is having some tea now.'

She did not offer McEvoy a cup, but left him waiting by
the door. The snow had vanished; there was a raw cold. She
called Fludd, as she made her way through to the kitchen;
heard him quit the sitting room, banging the door after him,
and greet McEvoy, and leave by the front door, exclaiming
as he did so over the wheelbarrow, its timeliness and conveni-
ence. She took her duster from the pantry, and went into the
sitting room which the curate had just vacated. Hurrying out
to McEvoy, he had placed his teacup carelessly on the mantel-
shelf. She reached out for it, and caught sight of herself in the
oval looking-glass. Her face was dead white, weary; her eyes
looked sore. But all the same, her wart had gone.

Father Angwin sat in the confessional; he felt safe there. He
drew his velvet curtain across the grille, and listened fearfully
to the thumps and scrapes from the nave. When the bishop
comes, he thought, perhaps I can take refuge here. He
wouldn't drag me out, would he? And do violence on me,
like Thomas à Becket and the knights?

Father's mood swung, between distress and jubilation,
between terror and mirth. Why should the bishop come, he
thought? There are no confirmations this coming year. He
shows no relish for our company. Unless malicious persons
like Purpit inform him of our schism, it can just go quietly on
its own way. Perhaps in time I might become an antipope.

He wished Miss Dempsey would bring him refreshments.

When the door opened, with a gentle creak, he jerked out
of his daydream. 'Fludd?'

'No. He is putting St Ambrose up.'

'Ah. My penitent.'

She knelt, with a soft rustle.

'How is your temptation?' He was afraid to hear the answer.

'A question,' she said.

'Yes. Go ahead.'

'Father, suppose a building collapsed. And in the ruins there are people buried. Can the priest give them absolution?'

'I think he could. Conditionally. If they were rescued, of course, they would have to confess their sins in the ordinary way.'

'Yes, I see.' A pause. 'Is there any kind of absolution you can give me?'

'Oh, my dear,' Father Angwin said. 'You are a girl who has stayed out all night. You could hardly make use of absolution now.'

It had not in fact occurred to Miss Dempsey to take refreshments to Father Angwin, for she did not know where to find him. She sat in her room, eating a caramel toffee. It was most unusual for her to suspend her activities in the course of the day. There was always something one could polish. And if ingenuity were really exhausted, one could turn mattresses.

But now she sat quietly, her eyes distant, crimping her gold toffee-paper into tiny folds. From time to time she touched her flawless lip. Certain lines ran through her head:

> Sweet Agnes, Holy Child,
> All purity;
> O may we undefiled
> Be pure as thee . . .

Swiftly, in her usual way, she twisted her paper into a ring. She took it reverently in her right hand, holding it between finger and thumb.

> Ready our blood to shed
> Rather than sin to wed . . .

She slid it on to her wedding finger. It looked admirable, she thought. One of the best rings she had achieved. It seemed a pity to waste it. She took it off and slipped it into the pocket of her pinny.

> Ready our blood to shed
> Rather than sin to wed.
> And forth as martyrs led
> To die like thee.

Chapter Nine

'I've got the key,' Sister Anthony whispered. 'She never normally lets it out of her possession. She was in a state this morning though. She's got a wart.' The nun tapped her face. 'Here. Here, on her lip. Ugly thing. Come up in the night like a mushroom. Cyril said to her, "Mother Purpiture, you want to get that looked at, I think it's cancer."'

'Oh, Sister Anthony,' Philly said, 'whatever shall I do?'

'Just follow me into the parlour.' Sister Anthony, her veil flapping, her elbows out, made sheepdog movements behind her back. 'Quick now, get a move on. I thought I'd never get her out of the place. How can I go on parish visits, she said, with this excrescence? In the end I told her there was a piece of gossip on Back Lane, some woman run away with her lodger. She can't resist a piece of gossip. She'll be out for the afternoon, going from house to house.'

'It goes dark by half past four,' Philly said.

'We'll have you out of here by then. By half past four you'll be on the train.'

Sister Anthony ushered her into the parlour, shut the door, and shoved a chair against it. Philomena regarded her, eyes wide.

'I can't put those clothes on. They're years old. They're older than me. There are clothes in there were put in before I was born.'

'Well, I can't credit this,' Sister Anthony said. 'I'd have thought you'd worry about being excommunicated, but all you care about is whether you're up with the modes.'

'That's not it at all. But everybody will notice me.'

'Nonsense. I'll transform you out of all recognition.'

'I'm not afraid will they recognize me. I'm afraid children will shout things and run after me down the street.'

'Well, what course do you favour?' the old nun demanded. 'I can't take you to the Co-op drapers to get outfitted. If you could beg borrow or steal from Agnes Dempsey, her skirts would be up round your thighs, you a great tall thing and she such a squat little woman.'

Sister Anthony bent over the chest and put the key in the lock. 'Come on, you filthy thing,' she said. 'Come on, you ingrate mechanism.' She gritted her teeth; cursed further. The lock gave. She turned back the lid.

'Well now,' she said, speculatively.

'You shouldn't be doing this for me,' Philly said.

'Nonsense.' Sister Anthony sniffed. 'I'm old. What can they do to me? They could put me on general post, I suppose. But I'd be glad to get away from here. I wouldn't mind if they shipped me out to the African missions. I'd rather live in a leper colony than spend another year with Purpit.'

Sister Anthony bent over and rummaged in the chest. 'Oh, by the way, speaking of Agnes Dempsey, she delivered this envelope for you.' She produced it from her pocket. 'I can't think what's in it. I hope it's a ten-shilling note. I can't spare you more than half a crown from the housekeeping without Purpit on my back saying I've lost it on a horse.'

Philly felt like a child, going on holiday. Or being togged up for a visit to relations. Leaving home for the first time.

But I can never come back, she thought. I know nothing except farms, convents, my mother's house. No convent in the world will take me in, after this afternoon. Even a farmer would show me the door; a Catholic farmer, that is. My mother would spit out at me across the street. Even my sister Kathleen wouldn't give me the time of day.

She took the envelope from Sister Anthony. Rattled it. It didn't really rattle. She opened it, carefully; nuns waste nothing. Even an envelope can sometimes be reused.

Miss Dempsey's ring rolled out on to her palm.

'Oh yes,' Sister Anthony said. 'What a mercy. You'll need a ring.'

'She must be barmy,' Sister Philomena said.

Her habit lay on one of the parlour chairs – folded, because she did not feel she could just drop it there. In disrobing before Sister Anthony, she had committed, she felt sure, ten or a dozen sins against holy modesty. Even to take off your clothes when you were by yourself could be a sin against holy modesty, if you didn't do it the right way. When she had joined the Order, she had learnt how to undress in a religious manner; to drop over her head the linen marquee of her nightgown, and wriggle out of her day clothes beneath it. Similarly, she had learnt to take a bath in her shift.

'What will you do with it? My habit?'

'I'll dispose of it in my own way.'

Now Sister Anthony felt for her more than ever. Out of her black drapings and her rolls of petticoats, standing shivering in the fireless parlour in her long linen drawers, she looked a pitiful beanpole, not at all the rough rural lass they were used to. She stood with her arms crossed over her breasts in a pose at once picturesque and gauche: going to God knows what.

'Twilfit or Excelsior?' Sister Anthony asked.

'Oh, I couldn't. I couldn't put on corsets. I've never worn corsets in my life.'

Sister Anthony was taken aback. 'Don't you have them in Ireland these days?'

'I shouldn't know how to manage. What if I wanted to go to the lavatory?'

'You'll have to have something, you know.' Sister Anthony felt around in the chest. 'Try this bust bodice. Come on now. Look lively.'

She couldn't get any sense of urgency into the girl. It was as if she were dressing up for charades. 'Either you may have my silk combinations,' she said, 'or you'll have to go in your drawers, please yourself.' She straightened up. 'Look, it's not too late, you know.' She pointed to the habit folded on the chair. 'You can climb back into that now, go straight up to Father Angwin, ask for absolution, say your penance, and forget about the whole thing.'

Philly turned a glance on her: large mild eyes. Then bent of her own accord over the chest: a swooning movement. She stood up, her white arms full of clothes. 'Anything,' she whispered. 'Anything will do. I can't stay here now. Purpit would know. She'd see it in my face. I'd rather be like St Felicity, eaten by the beasts in the circus.'

Finally Sister Anthony got her dressed. The blue serge suit seemed best, because warmest; it seemed no one had ever entered the convent in a top coat. The skirt dropped almost to her ankles, and its large waist swivelled round her small waist, washing about on her narrow frame. The jacket hung on her.

'I wish it were not such bad weather, you could take my straw hat,' Sister Anthony said. 'Such a lovely blue ribbon. I remember buying it, the summer before I came in.' She held it for a moment, and smoothed the ribbon with her pudgy flour-coloured fingers; then with sudden energy, sent it spinning back into the chest. She had produced from some other source a scratchy woollen headscarf of a kind of ersatz tartan, lime green and maroon. 'This will cover a multitude of sins,' she said. It was the kind of thing the Fetherhoughton women wore; perhaps a Child of Mary had mislaid it after a meeting, and Sister had snapped it up.

Shoes were a problem. Philly could just squeeze her feet into the smart little navy pair with the waisted heels; but to walk was another matter. She teetered about the parlour, wincing and crying out, 'Oh God,' she said. 'I've never had high heels. Oh, they do pinch.' She stopped. 'I suppose I could offer it up.'

'Not really,' Sister Anthony said. 'Not any more. There's no point in your offering anything up, is there?'

Philomena clung to the back of a chair. 'Will I be damned, Sister Anthony?'

'I should think so,' the nun said easily. 'Come on now, let me see you walk across the room.'

Philomena bit her underlip. She began; holding out her arms to aid her balance, like a performer on the high wire.

'I have to laugh,' Sister Anthony said, without doing so. 'If you wear those you'll end up in a casualty ward. I'll run down to school and fetch you a pair of the children's pumps.'

Philomena nodded. She saw the sense of this. 'Get different feet. Not two lefts.'

'And then if you wait a another minute, I'll go into the kitchen and make you up a parcel of provisions for the journey.'

'Oh, no Sister Anthony. Oh no, please don't trouble. I'm only going to Manchester.'

Sister Anthony's face said, you do not know where you will be going; and what can it matter to you if the bread gets a little stale? Think of the Pharaohs, their eternal picnics sealed in their tombs.

'Sit down, Sister. Rest your ankles.'

Obediently, Philly sat; then burst into tears. She had done well until now. But it was what the old woman had called her: 'Sister'. Soon she would never again hear that form of address.

Anthony regarded her thoughtfully. Then she took a clean,

folded handkerchief out of her pocket and passed it over. 'Keep it,' she said. 'I know you never have one of your own.' Strictly speaking, she knew, it was not hers to give. It was common property, which the Order had prescribed for her personal, temporary use. 'By the way,' she said. 'What was your name? Before you came into religion?'

Sister Philomena sniffed. 'Roisin.' She wiped her eyes. 'Roisin O'Halloran.'

Sister Anthony had said: wait until dusk. Now Roisin O'Halloran fled like an animal over the dark ground. In that moment, in that heart-stopping moment before Anthony let her out of the back door – when she stood with her Gladstone bag in her hand, like a runner on his mark – she had heard in the passage, approaching, a little clicking noise. It was Polycarp, Cyril and Ignatius Loyola; and as they bustled along, their rosary beads clinked together, and made a noise like the gnashing of teeth.

She ran; but when she had gained the path to the allotments, she stopped and looked back, conserving her breath. Four o'clock struck by the church clock. She saw them clustered, all three, at an upper, open window. She wanted to shrink into the scrubby bushes, the standing pools. Then she saw that they were waving their handkerchiefs; dipping them up and down, with a curiously sedate, formal motion.

She turned around fully, her bag clasped before her in two hands, a skinny, dowdy figure in her strange clothes. She looked up at the convent, its many small windows, its smoke-blackened stone; beyond it were the slates of the church roof, slick with the air's moisture, and above the church the glowering terraces, leaf-mulched, slippery, the jungle of the north. The mill-windows of Fetherhoughton were lit up; the smoke from the tall chimneys had faded into the darkening sky, but factory furnaces burnt, dull slow jewels of the year's end. She raised her arm, waved. The handkerchiefs bobbed up and down. A voice carried to her.

'Send us an epistle,' said Polycarp.

'Send us a food parcel,' said Cyril.

'Send us –' said Ignatius Loyola; but she never found out what it was because she had turned again, and loped onwards, towards the first stile. When she looked back again, they were still there, but well out of earshot now; handkerchiefs and faces were indistinguishable in the gloom.

Roisin O'Halloran fled like an animal over the dark ground, observed – from a vantage point on Back Lane – by Mother Purpiture.

In the presbytery, the telephone rang. 'I have the bishop for you,' whispered the sycophant: across the wires.

'One moment,' said Agnes Dempsey. She placed the telephone receiver on the hall table, went down the hall and tapped on the sitting-room door, 'It's him,' she said. 'Will I get Father Fludd to talk to him?'

Father Angwin raised his hands, poised them like a pianist over the keys; he let them fall on to the arms of his chair, and bounced to his feet. 'No,' he said, 'I am responsible.' He opened the door, and glanced swiftly up and down the hall, as if the bishop might be lurking in the shadows. 'Where is Father Fludd?'

'In his room. I think I heard him go up.'

'I thought I heard him come down. Still, both are possible.' Both at once, he thought.

Agnes stood by his elbow when he took up the receiver. Formerly, she would have crept back to the kitchen. She had grown bolder; a smile played continually about the corners of her mouth, as if she had seen something gratifying, or learnt something that pleased her.

Father Angwin held the receiver at a good distance from his ear. For a while he listened to the bishop prosing on. She caught a phrase here and there: *something in the way of a social for the younger end . . . the altar boys . . . a record hop, as I believe our American friends call it.* 'He doesn't know,' Father mouthed at Agnes. 'Doesn't know yet.'

'That Purpiture,' Agnes mouthed back, 'has gone Upstreet. She might go in the Post Office and telephone him. Sister Polycarp said she took coins with her. She doesn't shop, so what else could it be for?'

'She's my mortal enemy,' Father Angwin whispered. 'I wouldn't put it past her.' He turned back to the bishop. 'I was wondering, Aidan, could you help me out with a question put to me by a parishioner?'

There was a frigid pause, on the line; Miss Dempsey wondered why Father had used the bishop's christian name, for he had never done so before. Father's tone, she thought had a meaningful mysterious jocularity. 'It's about a friend of his, a doctor,' he continued. 'This doctor has human bones in his possession, and got them when he was a student in a Protestant country. It may have been Germany, because my parishioner has another friend, some Hun, who is anxious to go to confession but speaks no English, and I hardly know whether we should have an interpreter or some other arrangement?'

Miss Dempsey strained to hear. It seemed that the bishop made no reply or a muffled one.

'No, don't rush yourself,' Father said, 'give it your leisurely consideration, it's a nice point. Really, Aidan, you wouldn't credit it, I am beginning to encounter the most bizarre difficulties, circumstances that one does not come across in forty years as a parish priest. There is also some confusion here in Fetherhoughton about the minutiae of the Church's teaching on the Lenten fast, and we were wondering, out of the depth of your accumulated experience, would you advise us?'

There was a long pause; the bishop said, in a tone that lacked his habitual fire: 'Now look here . . .'

Miss Dempsey missed his next words. Then she heard,

'. . . just doing my job. Duty of obedience. Task laid upon me . . . only a young feller.' Father Angwin hugged the receiver, and smiled. 'Times change,' the bishop said. '. . . hardly reason to be ashamed . . .'

'But you are ashamed, aren't you?' Father Angwin said. 'Why, man, if this were to get out, then where two or three modern bishops are gathered together, you would lose your credibility entirely.'

'I will be upon you, Angwin, one day this week. Count upon it.'

'And I will be upon you,' muttered the priest, as he put the receiver down. 'I shall have your liver on toast. Agnes, warn Fludd.'

'Warn him?' The word stood out, shockingly, claiming attention for itself.

'Yes. Warn him that the bishop may turn up any time.'

'How shall I warn him?' Agnes said carefully.

'You may call up the stairs.'

'Shall I not go up?'

'To call will be sufficient.'

'Yes. I should not discommode him by tapping at his door.'

'He might be at prayer.'

'I should not like to interrupt him.'

They looked at each other. 'I did not positively see him go up,' said Miss Dempsey.

'Or come down.'

'I would have to assume he was up there.'

'It would be a fair assumption. A reasonable man might make it.'

'Or woman.' Miss Dempsey went to the foot of the stairs. 'Father Fludd,' she called softly. 'Father Fludd?'

'Don't expect an answer,' Angwin said.

'He would not break off his devotions.'

'But we can suppose he has heard.'

They knew, though, that the upper storey was empty, quite as certainly as they had ever known anything. Ashes rustled softly through the grate; on the walls twisted Christs continued dying; in the church grounds, yellow leaves floated in darkening air, birds huddled in the trees of the terraces, and worms turned.

'Shall I put the kettle on?' Agnes said.

'No, I am going to have a glass of whisky and read a book that a parishioner has lent me.'

Has left me, he almost said. He bit the word back in time. Miss Dempsey nodded. Fludd is in his room, of course, praying. Philomena is in her convent, of course, sweeping out the kitchen passage under the direction of Sister Anthony. Everyone is where they should be; or we may collude in pretending so. And God's in his heaven? Very bloody likely, Father Angwin thought.

He sat with his book, turning it over in his hands; the stained, battered yellow-brown cover. *Faith and Morals for the Catholic Fireside: A Question-box for the Layman.* Published Dublin, 1945. *Nihil Obstat: Patrilius Dargan.* Here was the imprimatur of the Archbishop of Dublin himself, with a little cross printed by his name.

She got it all out of this, he thought, all our conversations: what a treasury of scruple, what a cache of conservative principle. Here it is, the old faith in its entirety; the dear old faith, with no room for doubt or dissent. The rules of fasting and abstinence; no mention of record hops. Diatribes against impure thoughts; no mention of relevance. And just here on the tattered spine the general editor's name, none other than The Revd (as he was then) Aidan Raphael Croucher, Doctor of Divinity: the bishop in person.

I shall store it under my pillow, Father Angwin resolved; it will keep me in gibes for years to come. How I shall persecute the fellow with his past opinions; bringing up one question or another, intruding them into casual conversation, until his terror of me is complete. *May dripping be used for pastry, or is it allowed only for frying fish?* He has got up to his bishopric on the back of such questions. None of us can know what we will come to; but some of us cannot even remember how we began.

Question: *Why is fortune-telling permitted at Catholic bazaars?* Answer: The practice is not to be encouraged, many healthier amusements could be substituted. Question: *Is it right for the Catholic Church to pass a collection-box during Sunday evening Lent services?* It is always right, sometimes it is advisable and frequently it is necessary.

I knew she was reading it off a paper, Father said to himself. I suspected she had all the answers. There was a name written in pencil on the fly-leaf, in a round schoolgirl's hand. *Dymphna O'Halloran.* This is all she brought from Ireland, he thought; and I supposed it was one of the convent's books. This is all she brought from Ireland and now she has left it to me. He thumbed his way back to the preface. *Divine Revelation, coupled with two thousand years' experience has made the Church an incomparable teacher in matters of human conduct. There is not a walk of life, a personal activity, a private or public occasion, on which our Holy Mother is not able to teach, encourage, warn or advise us, from the deep knowledge she has of the human heart and mind, and their strange modes of action.*

Two thousand years' experience, Father Angwin said to himself. It is an awesome thought. He reached blindly for his whisky glass. His fingers closed on it, he brought it to his mouth. He tasted it and held it off, he held it up to the light with his eyes screwed up and looked at it. It had the appearance, the colour, the outer properties, yet it was not whisky; it was water. Oh, Fludd, he thought, you sorcerer's apprentice, you've gone and got it wrong this time. You've worked a miracle in reverse. You've doused the celestial fire, you've taken the divine and made it merely human, you've exchanged the spirit for damp, warm flesh.

But meanwhile, Perpetua scrambled across country. I shall get her at the station, she thought. She did not stop to think what a figure she cut, galloping and puffing, her habit bunched up in her fists to clear the ground, her lace-ups scuffed and a hole torn in her stocking, her crucifix on its cord bouncing against the place where laywomen have their bosoms. She ran at a peculiar crouch, pausing every so often to stand upright, massage her ribs and sight her quarry. On the tops of stiles she hovered, to scan the country. The beast was not now in sight; but I shall corner her on the platform, Purpit thought.

She had time to notice, as she ran, the white streamer that looped and snaked on the wind, fastened to a fence pole; and even as she ran, she thought there was something familiar about it, something faintly ecclesiastical, something that made her want to stop and genuflect. She conquered the inclination. I shall trap her on the platform, she thought, and drag her back, I shall drag her down Upstreet in full view, and before night falls I shall have pulled those clothes from her back and locked her in her cell to wait until the bishop comes, and then we shall see, and then we shall see, then we shall see about the degraded minx.

Her heart pounded and roared in her ears, under the folds of her veil. She did not doubt she had the advantage; the station path was but a sprint away. As she turned downhill, the evening seemed to close in over the allotments behind her: that rolling darkness, rolling down from the moors. From the hen-houses, a single point of light gleamed: as it might be, the tip of a lighted cigarette.

She had almost gained the station path, when a figure rose up before her, out of the bushes, and blocked her path. She stopped, and stared, eyes popping. It was a figure she knew, a form she knew; yet subject to change, to a transformation that froze her blood. 'Oh, horrible,' said Mother Purpit: caught half-way over the final stile.

Roisin O'Halloran stood on the platform, her Gladstone bag held before her in her hands; prepared, as if she did not know how quickly the train might come upon her. She stared down the track. Her tartan headscarf flapped boisterously, and her ungloved hands with their paper ring were blue around the knuckles.

Across the moors that train must come, but what if snow had fallen in Sheffield today? What if Woodhead was blocked, what if a blizzard was brewing? Snowploughs out. Ice on the points. Sheep buried alive on the moors. Men in mufflers and spiked boots, crystals in their moustaches, going about with spades to dig people out. She pictured herself huddled in the waiting room, on the bench into which the Netherhoughtonians had cut their runes; she imagined the voice of the station-master, 'No trains out tonight.'

She had no watch. She did not know when the train ought to come. She had bought her ticket with her head bowed, in a false voice. She was like a parcel, she thought, addressed but not posted. She had felt the ticket-man's eyes on her back. She did not dare ask him, what time will the train come? She had hoped for a public notice of some kind. But no doubt if there had been one, the people from Nether-houghton would have come by night and torn it down.

In her shyness, her confusion, her haste, she had not asked Father Fludd, what time will the train come and carry me away? She had only heard him say, *I will be after you. When you reach the other end, wait in the baggage hall. Confide in no one.* It occurred to her that this man, this false priest, the impostor with whom she would soon embark on the dreadful Act, was a mystery she hardly dared address, a man whom she did not know. I do not know God, she thought. But I always Trusted in Him.

Roisin O'Halloran put down her bag, and rubbed her hands together to restore the circulation. A question drifted up to her mind: *Some years ago I intended going to a certain town by train. I happened to meet a man who had a ticket for that place, but who changed his mind and decided not to travel. He gave me his ticket and I travelled with it. Was there any injustice to the railway company?*

What was the answer? She stood frowning, trying to recall it; bending her furious thoughts to anything but the matter in hand. *There is no injustice. The railway companies do not insist on personal identification. They are satisfied if every traveller has the ticket required for the journey.*

The platform, by some merciful dispensation, had been deserted when she arrived, but now she saw, out of the corner of her eye, that a man had arrived. He stood behind her, a little distance away. She hunched her shoulders into the navy jacket, and put a hand up to draw her scarf further over her head. Let it be some Protestant, she prayed, someone who wouldn't know me. Then she thought, what's the use of praying for that sort of thing? Or any sort of thing at all?

He must, she thought, be examining with some curiosity my peculiar-looking back. The skin of her neck crawled; almost as if the man were Fludd. She began to turn her head; slowly but inexorably, as if it were subject to a magnetic attraction.

And yes, of course he was staring at her. Their eyes met; shocked, she jerked her gaze away, as if she had seen a corpse on the track.

As the man was Mr McEvoy, he could hardly have failed to recognize her; but he did not speak. The wind tore through her jacket and sliced her through to the bone; it got under her skirt, and barrelled it out around her legs. She turned her eyes down and kept them on her gym pumps; one right, one left.

Then at last the train appeared, a dot in the distance, so

faint in the gathering darkness that she could hardly be sure it was there. For seconds it seemed to stick absurdly, going neither forwards nor back; then, when she saw that it was growing larger, she stepped forward to the edge of the platform, and raised her face, caught in the orange glow of the station lamps.

Only when the train drew in did Mr McEvoy step up beside her. She was trembling all over. 'Sister?' he said, in a low voice. He offered his arm. Her fingertips rested on it; she had some thought of fending him off. He swung open the carriage door for her. 'Don't alarm yourself,' he said. 'I am only travelling as far as Dinting, just the few stops. I shall pretend not to know you. I am the soul of discretion.'

'Then get away,' she hissed. 'Leave me alone.'

'I only wish to be of assistance,' McEvoy said. 'Somebody must hand you your bag and see that you have a seat facing the engine. And you know what they say, Sister. Better the devil you know.'

With a simper, Mr McEvoy placed her bag on the rack. A door slammed. A railwayman gave a wild inchoate shout. Flags waved. And a moment later they were off, rattling across the points to Manchester, her defloration and the Royal and Northwestern Hotel.

Chapter Ten

The Royal and Northwestern Hotel had been designed by a pupil of Sir Gilbert Scott in a moment of absent-mindedness, and when Roisin O'Halloran entered its portals she felt uneasily at home. She turned to her companion; 'Like church,' she whispered. The foyer had a marmoreal chill. Behind a mahogany desk, curiously carved, proportioned like an altar, stood a sallow-faced personage, with the bloodless lips and sunken cheeks of a Vatican City intriguer; and he proffered them a great volume, like a chained Bible, and with a pallid, spatulate fingertip indicated the place for Fludd to put his superscription. When this was done the personage frowned at it, and then smiled a thin wintry smile, like a martyr whose hangman has cracked a joke: 'We have a nice quiet room, Doctor,' he said.

Doctor, thought Roisin. So you are up to your old tricks. Fludd caught her eye and smiled faintly, but with more merriment than the personage. The personage eased open a great drawer, like a vestment chest, and selected among the keys; then he drew one out, and presented it. In this way, with the same caution, St Peter selects a key for one of heaven's more inconspicuous doors, and hands it to one of the elect who has only just scraped in.

'They're not over-friendly,' she whispered, on her way to the lift. But then, she thought, it's not us perhaps, hotel keepers are like it. She thought of Mrs Monaghan, at Monaghan's Hotel, grumbling if she had to turn out her back room for a commercial traveller. Dymphna used to wash up at Monaghan's Hotel; and later, it was said, make herself available in the bar parlour.

When she thought of this, Roisin O'Halloran's cheeks burned. Then something more obvious struck her. 'Is it me?' she mouthed at Fludd. 'Is it the funny way I look?'

The iron grilles of the lift clattered behind them, trapping them in. Fludd's hand crept over her cold hand. With a lurch, the machine began to move; an unseen force drew them upward, up into the bowels of the place. As they vanished into the darkness between floors, for one instant she saw, beyond the bars, Perpetua's face; it was a mask of fury, and with a snort of jealousy and rage the decapitated vision reached out, and spouted clawing hands, and wormed her fingers between the metalwork.

There was a wardrobe to put your clothes. It was a novelty to her. At home they had only a chest of drawers, and an old musty cupboard in the wall. In a convent, well, you don't need such things.

'Are you going to unpack your bag?' Fludd said. 'Hang things up?'

'I could hang up my costume,' she said, 'if I took it off.' As she looked around her, naked pleasure shone from her face. 'I could hang up my frock. I've brought a frock. It belonged to Sister Polycarp. It's got a sailor collar. You've never seen such a frock.'

Fludd turned away. She was a sore, sharp, grievous temptation; now that he saw her here, in a warm room, amid furnishings, he saw her glow with gentleness and hope. She had never been part of his plans; no woman had, no fleshly tie of any sort. Some spoke of the *soror mystica*, companion in a man's work; but to him it had seemed always that women were leeches on knowledge, sappers of scholarship. Still, he thought: other times, other manners.

Other times, other manners. Philomena took off her jacket. She folded it and laid it on the bed. The room was cavernous, stuffy; some great engine, hidden beneath the floor, chuffed out heat. The bed was made with stiff white linen; the eiderdown was plump and purple, shining and silky, the kind of quilt a Papal legate might have. On the wall, cabbage roses bloomed; blue roses, the white space between them pickled a yellow-brown by the tobacco smoke of previous guests. There was a washbasin in the corner, behind a screen, and upon it a cold cake of green soap, and by it a white towel, with the hotel's initials sewn on it in a florid scarlet script.

'Must I take my other clothes off too?' the girl said.

When Roisin O'Halloran lay at last beneath the bedsheets, her naked body rigid in their glacial embrace, her thoughts were of her own ineptitude, of how easily everything could have gone awry. Fludd had been wearing, when she met him at the station, a suit made of tweed, and so when the passengers came off the train from Fetherhoughton she had failed to see him, because she was looking for clerical black. She had not told him this, nor how she had panicked in the moment before he hurried up to her and kissed her cheek and took the bag from her hand. The mistake seemed to add a further dimension to her foolishness; was there ever a woman in the history of the world who ran off with a man she could not recognize?

Now Fludd undressed modestly, his back turned to her. She watched him take his handkerchief from his pocket, and lay it on the dressing table, like a white nest – into which he dropped his small change. She thought, I am seeing what other women see every day. Then he had gestured to her – his torso transparently white, like a saint's robe – that she should turn back the covers for him, and switch off the lamp. Reduced to a dim outline, he shed the rest of his clothes, and they fell on to the floor, beside hers. Gliding over the Axminster without a sound, he arrived at the bed.

When she reached out, and folded her arms around his body, she felt that she was closing them on air. Her eyes opened wide, her lips pressed together in fear of pain, she fell back against the pillows, her neck outstretched. She turned her head and watched the wall, the curtain, their shadows moving across the wall. Every possession is a loss, Fludd said. But equally, every loss is a possession.

Later, while she slept, her cropped head buried deep in the feather pillow, Fludd slipped from the bed and stood watching her, and listening to the sounds of the city at night. He heard the mournful shunting and the calls of trains, the feet of night porters on the stairs, the singing of a drunk in St Peter's Square: he heard ragged breathing from a hundred rooms, the morse chattering of ships at sea, the creak and scrape of the pivot as angels turned the earth. He splashed water on his face and rubbed it with the white towel; then he crawled back into the bed beside her, and fell asleep as his eyes closed, overcome by the power of his dreams.

The next day, Roisin O'Halloran didn't want to go out. She was ashamed of her clothes; and of her hair too, without the checked headscarf. Fludd said he would take her to a department store and she could get something in the fashion, but she hardly felt she could face a saleswoman; they would trick her out of her money, she felt, turn her out in some clownish way.

For years she had never thought of her body; swathed inside her habit, it seemed to have developed its own secret way of life. You put one foot in front of the other and that was how you walked. You rolled, you shambled, the habit hiding your gait. You got along as best you might; but now you must study moving. Last night she had caught a glimpse of women in the hotel corridors, stepping along on bird-like legs. They were alive with a contained tension, their eyes smiling under painted brows; in the echoing cathedral nave of the foyer, they pulled on gloves with tiny pecking movements of their fingers. They snapped open their handbags and fumbled inside them, and took out little handkerchiefs, and powder compacts.

'I ought to have all that,' she said, incredulous. 'Lipsticks.'

'And scent,' Fludd said.

'Face-powder.'

'Furs,' Fludd said.

He tried to coax her out of the room, out of the bed; but she sat up against the pillows, with the linen sheets, which had crackled with starch last night and now felt limp and damp, pulled up to her chin. She could not explain to him that she felt that she already had new clothes, that with the loss of her virginity she had put on another skin. People say, 'loss', she reflected, but they do not know what innocence is like. Innocence is a bleeding wound without a bandage, a wound that opens with every casual knock from casual passers-by. Experience is armour; and she felt already clad.

She had woken at five, the convent hour, and found herself ravenously hungry. She had to contain and soothe her hunger in the dark, lying beside Fludd's sleeping form. She could not see him breathe; sometimes she leant over him to see if he were dead.

At seven o'clock Fludd woke up. He ordered breakfast to be sent to their room. She pulled the sheets over her head and hid when the knock came at the door, and for minutes afterwards she cowered there in case the hotel person should have forgotten something and come back again. Fludd plied the EPNS teapot; she heard the little clink the china made, when cup was set on saucer. 'Sit up,' he said. 'Here is an egg for you.'

She had it on her knees, on a tray. She had never had breakfast in bed before, but she had read about it in books. It seemed a dangerous business, keeping the tray wedged just so between ribs and navel, not breathing too much, not moving your legs. Fludd picked up sugar lumps in little tongs, and dropped them into her tea, and stirred it for her; each cup and saucer had its own spoon.

'Just try it,' Fludd urged, as she half-sat, half-lay, looking dubiously at what was put before her. 'Let me butter some toast for you, and you can have marmalade too. Eat up your egg, it will make you strong.'

She took up her cutlery; hesitated. 'Which is the better side of the egg to cut into, do you think?'

'It's a matter of personal preference.'

'But which do you *think*?' she persisted.

'Doesn't matter what I think. You must do as you like. There's no rule, you see.'

'At the convent we didn't get eggs. We got porridge.'

'You must have had eggs at home. In Ireland. I thought you were from off a farm.'

'We had eggs on the farm, yes, but not to eat. To sell. At least,' she added, after some thought, 'we did eat them sometimes, but not so often that you worked out your own way of going on.'

Fludd's egg was already pithed, demolished. She hadn't seen him open it up, much less eat it, and yet she could swear that for five minutes she hadn't taken her eyes from his face.

Later they needed more food. When she unpacked her Gladstone bag she realized that Sister Anthony had secreted, in the folds of Sister Polycarp's sailor dress, a number of small, gritty buns. She thought they might subsist on these, but Fludd had other ideas.

He sent downstairs again. A large oval plate came, with a doily on it, with very small sandwiches with the crusts cut off; and there was another plate, which had buns with frosted icing, some white and some pink, topped with angelica leaves and tiny candied flowers.

The day passed. She was tired, so tired. Fludd took the trays away, and she leant back against the pillows. All the weariness of her convent years, all the weariness of her early-rising childhood, seemed to visit her at once, like a tribe of unexpected relatives. 'I could drink sleep,' she said, 'I could eat it, I could roll around in my dreams like a pig in mud.' When she was awake, they talked, in a desultory way; she told him her childhood, but he did not tell her his. Later, he telephoned for wine. Money seemed no problem to Fludd.

And the wine – a sweetish, straw-coloured wine, the first she had tasted – went to her head. She closed her eyes for a moment and allowed herself to think of next day. Fludd said it would be all right about her hair, that if she liked he would go himself to Paulden's on Market Street, and buy her a silk scarf, which they would arrange around her head in some artistic way; or if she preferred, he said, some kind of smart toque. But she did not know what was a toque; she kept silent on the matter.

When she opened her eyes again, Fludd was standing by the window, looking down into the street. People were on their way home from work, he said, hurrying to Exchange Station and to Victoria. It was raining, he said, and the people were packed on the pavements under their bobbing umbrellas, like lines of black beetles on the march.

Fludd stood watching them, leaning with his outstretched arm propping the wall. His head drooped on to his arm, and he nuzzled it with his forehead and cheek, like a cat against a sofa. 'I feel trapped, in this room,' he said. 'Tomorrow we must certainly go out.'

But it is only one day, she wanted to protest. Twenty-seven hours ago, she had been in the convent parlour, dressing herself under the directions of Sister Anthony. Twenty-four hours ago – perhaps a little less – they had entered this room.

Elsewhere, life went on as before; bells rang, the convent kept its hours. Whatever had Purpit said, when she returned from her parish visits and found her gone? Had she known at once, or was it at chapel she had missed her, or at the evening soup collation? Had the others made some excuse, to hide her absence as long as possible? Had they lied for her? Had they imperilled their immortal souls?

She twisted Miss Dempsey's paper ring round and round on her finger. It really was a skilful construction. Already, when she thought about it, Purpit's face was growing dim: as if time and experience had consumed her, burnt her like a wax doll.

Presently Fludd, tired of watching the office workers, rejoined her in the bed.

Miss Dempsey, that little smile still hovering about her lips, brought in the tea-tray. In Fetherhoughton, of course, the weather was worse than in town. The bishop sat blocking the fire, looking chilly and shrunken, a shadow of himself.

He had not been into the church yet; he was not pious, except upon provocation. When he did go in, he would simply leap to the conclusion that his orders had been ignored. The statues, upon their plinths, were as good as new, each one with its iron circle of candles; for the Children of Mary had washed them down, buffed and polished them and made good any minor damage with their paintbrushes.

Father Angwin toyed with a bourbon biscuit. What will you say, Aidan Raphael Croucher, when you conclude your fiat has been ignored? If you are wise, and do not want your former opinions blazoned about the diocese, you will smile at me politely and say nothing. And in the future, you will deal more respectfully with me.

'Absconded,' the bishop said, in a flat voice. 'Dear, oh dear. Modern manners.'

'Absconded, perhaps. Or done away with.'

'Oh, dear God,' said the bishop. 'Do you tell me?' He could see repercussions from this.

'I am expecting the police, tomorrow at first light, to dig about the grounds. An Inspector was here. He walked about behind the garage and saw a place where the ground had been disturbed.'

'Is it possible?' The bishop's hand trembled; his tea slopped over into his saucer. 'Who would want to do away with a nun?'

'Suspicion would fall upon the people from Nether-houghton,' Father Angwin said, 'seeking a virgin for their rites.'

He recalled the parishioner who, with trembling hand, had come to him after early Mass, and handed him a brown paper bag. In that bag was a part of Fludd's vestments – his stole, found tied to a fence post on the allotments. Rumours of the curate's disappearance were already about the parish, and there were those who had opined, when dawn broke over the hen-houses, and in the early light the silken streamer became visible from Back Lane, that he had placed it there as a flag of distress; others, quicker to conclude against their neighbours, believed that a drunken and cannibalistic raiding party from the Old Oak and the Ram had carried off the young man in the small hours from the unfortified presbytery, and now flew his stole as a banner of triumph.

Father Angwin was perfectly confident that nothing ill had befallen Fludd, but he could not say so; for then he would be obliged to account for him, produce him. But he had tried to assuage the parish's fears, earlier that day, by encouraging the rationalist tendency: and by laying the blame for any malfeasance in the district at the door of a certain stranger, who had been about the place unremarked until, the railway-men said, he had turned up at the station at six o'clock yesterday evening and purchased a single ticket to town. The railwaymen remembered the stranger's tweed suit; but as for his features, they were not able to give even the vaguest information.

But thankfully, the bishop had not yet mentioned Fludd. He was preoccupied with convent affairs. 'Please God she may be discovered safe and sound,' he said. 'She can be brought back if we can discover her. We could put out some story about amnesia. It would prevent the giving of scandal.'

'The Protestants will make hay with it,' Father Angwin remarked.

'You sit there, Father, and look so cool,' the bishop burst out. He slammed his cup and saucer down on to the table, spilling some tea over Agnes's red chenille cloth. 'You look so cool, after telling me a professed sister has run off from the convent, that Mother Perpetua has burst into flames while on her parish visits – tell me, what did she say, she must have said something before they took her away, you do not have a nun, and a convent superior at that, just suddenly set on fire!'

Father Angwin picked a crumb from his knee, fastidious, making no immediate reply. He remembered how a wondering Sister Anthony had brought the news: 'Mother Purpit has burnt up, wart and all.' The bishop, he noticed, washed his fists together in an agitated way, right hand in left palm, then left hand in right.

'She was in no condition for much conversation,' he said. 'The stretcher-bearers said she mumbled something about a low blue flame, creeping towards her over the grass . . . They could make nothing of it.'

'She must be questioned at the hospital.'

'They say she is not fit. Agnes telephoned this morning and they said she had spent a comfortable night. That is what hospitals say, Agnes tells me, when you are nearly dead. I spoke to the ward sister myself and they said that she was not much disfigured but that she had had a shock. They couldn't think when she would be able to explain events. I

think you underestimate, Aidan, the seriousness of the con-
flagration. As you know, she was only put out by the good
offices of a passing tobacconist.'

'The tobacconist must be questioned. He is a Catholic,
you say?'

'A prominent parishioner. Very active in the Men's Fellowship.'

'Oh dear, dear,' said the bishop again. 'What a mercy he
was passing. It is a bad business, this, Angwin, it is a very
bad business. It looks very bad, and it all comes back on me.'

'Do you think it was a diabolic manifestation?' Angwin
asked.

'Tosh,' the bishop replied, with a flash of spirit.

Angwin gave him a warning look. 'Nuns have had their
troubles in that line,' he said. 'Demons threw St Catherine of
Siena into the fire many a time. They pulled her off her
horse, and tipped her into a freezing river head first. Sister
Mary Angelica, a nun from Evreux, was followed for two
years by a devil in the form of a green scaly dog.' He paused,
enjoying the effect he was making. 'A Mother Agnes, a
Dominican, was attacked by the devil in the form of a pack
of wolves. Saint Margaret Mary had her seat pulled from
under her as she sat before the convent fire. Three other nuns
testified in writing that they saw the holy person repeatedly
and by supernatural forces dumped on her backside.'

'There must be some other explanation,' the bishop said
pathetically.

'You mean a more modern explanation? A more relevant
one? Some ecumenical kind of a reason why it occurred?'

'Do not torment me, Angwin,' the bishop wailed. 'I am a
man sorely tried. I feel there must have been some chemical
reaction that caused it.'

'The devil is a great chemist,' Angwin said.

'Of course there are cases of it, people bursting into flames,
though I have never heard of it in a nun. There is a case of it

in one of the novels of Dickens, is there not? And that fellow has written a study of it, what do you call him, the fellow with the deerstalker and the violin?'

'I think perhaps you mean Mr Arthur Conan Doyle,' Father Angwin said. 'I did not know you read such sensational stuff. More tea?'

'They call it spontaneous combustion,' the bishop said. He looked wild-eyed at the thought.

'Combustion, certainly,' Father Angwin agreed. Personally he doubted the spontaneity of it; he had doubted it at once, when he learnt that McEvoy was on the scene. It is a wise man, he thought, who can tell the firefighter from the arsonist.

In his room at the Royal and Northwestern, while women in cocktail dresses tripped downstairs to drink gin in the tomb-like bar, Fludd turned over in bed. Roisin O'Halloran stirred herself from her doze. She reached out, trailing her fingertips across his chest, and switched on the bedside lamp. It was eight o'clock. They had not drawn the curtains, and a street-lamp shone in, lending a parched, sub-lunary whiteness to the room; the lamp's silk fringe cast a pattern of massive loops on to the wall by the wardrobe.

She sat up. She was beginning to feel a stiffness in the muscles of her inner thighs. Fludd said that they were muscles she had not used before. He said she should go along the corridor and take a hot bath, and put in perfumed bath oil, and revel in the steam and heat and spotless white tiles.

He rolled on to his back now; his eyes were open, looking into the darkness. 'It must be time for dinner,' he said. 'We could go down.'

'Yes,' she said. Suddenly – perhaps it had happened in her last bout of sleep – she had stopped caring so much about her clothes, her hair, the inadequacies her new life exposed to view. She sat up, and now that she had stopped caring, let the sheets fall away. Her throat and the fine skin of her chest were mottled and glowing, and she brushed a hand across her breasts, which had begun to ache. How heavy they were; she cupped them for a moment. 'I must have a brassiere,' she said. 'Tomorrow.'

'For tonight you must do without,' Fludd said. 'I suppose if I were a man of great ardour I would suggest that we stayed here for the rest of the night, but they are said to have French food in this place, and I should like to eat some. You will come, won't you?'

'Yes.' She leant over to put on her lamp, and sat huddled in the wreck of the bed, her ankles crossed and her knees drawn up to her chest. 'Before we get up,' she said, 'read my palm again. You saw a star on it, didn't you? Will you look for it again?'

'It is too dim in here,' said Fludd.

'Later then?'

'Perhaps. Downstairs.'

The bishop seemed to have got paralysed. He sat in silence, looking into the fire, as if he were wondering about its nature. Father Angwin did not know whether he ought to get Agnes to cook something for them both. He wondered what she had bought that day when she went Upstreet, and indeed whether, considering that Upstreet hummed with rumour and speculation, she had remembered to buy anything at all.

'We might have a little something,' he suggested to the bishop. 'I could ask my housekeeper to see about it. Whatever she has got, there should be ample for both of us. Father Fludd cannot join us, I'm afraid, he is dining elsewhere tonight.'

He had got excuses ready, to cover for his curate's disappearance: Fludd has been bidden forth by a member of the Men's Fellowship, whose sister is visiting from the country and has brought a rabbit for a pie. Better still: Father Fludd has been invited to a funeral tea. He is out comforting the bereaved, and they will be having cold boiled ham.

The bishop looked up. 'Fludd?' he said. 'Who is Fludd? I know nothing of Fludd.'

Father Angwin heard what the bishop said. He did not answer. It was a moment before the implications came home to him. He sat very still. He was not surprised, when he thought about it: he was not surprised at all.

What was it the angel said, when he explained himself to Tobias? 'I seemed indeed to eat and drink with you; but I use an invisible meat and drink, which cannot be seen by men.'

The waiter put a damask napkin in her lap; it was as large as a small tablecloth. She wore the little white muslin dress, with the sailor collar; Fludd had helped her into it, and told her she looked pretty, and now, old-fashioned as it was, its airy summer skirt caressed her calves beneath the table. And the bodice was decent, she thought. Not that she much cared.

A second waiter lit a candle on the table; others moved in the shadows, pushing trolleys and pulling out diners' chairs. The waiters had stiff white jackets buttoned over their hollow chests, and their faces were the ancient, sharp faces of juvenile delinquents.

'In my former life,' Fludd said, 'I never had much to do with women. Now I see what I was missing.'

'What do you mean, your former life? Do you mean when you were impersonating a doctor?'

Fludd looked up, a piece of fruit he called melon speared on his fork and poised in the air.

'Who told you I did that?'

'You. You as good as told me.'

'You don't understand an analogy, do you?'

'No.' She looked down at her plate, ashamed. She could make nothing of the melon; it tasted to her like sucked fingers, flesh dissolved in water. 'I like everything to be just what it is, I suppose. That's why I hated it when I had the stigmata. I didn't understand it. Nobody had crucified me. I didn't understand why I had to have it at all.'

'Don't talk about that,' Fludd said. 'That's all over and done with now. You're going to get a fresh start.'

The waiter came and took their plates away. 'My palm,' the girl said. 'You're forgetting. You said you'd read it, if I'd come down.'

She held it out under the candle. 'Once is enough,' Fludd said.

'No, tell me again. I didn't listen properly the first time. I want to know my destiny.'

'I can't tell you that.'

'I thought it was written in my lines. I thought you believed in it.'

'Patterns can alter,' Fludd said. 'A soul is a thing in a state of flux. You fate is mutable. Your will is free.' He reached across the table, and tapped once with his forefinger, urgently, in the palm of her hand. 'Roisin O'Halloran, listen to me now. It is true that, in a way, I can tell the future. But not in the way you think. I can make you a map. I can indicate to you a choice of turnings. But I cannot travel the route on your behalf.'

She dropped her head. 'Are you afraid?' Fludd said.

'Yes.'

'Good. That's the way it should be. Nothing is achieved without proper fear.' Her mouth trembled. 'You don't understand,' he said tiredly.

'Help me then.' Her eyes pleaded: animal eyes. 'I don't know who you are. I don't know where you come from. I don't know where you might take me.'

At other tables, the sated diners rose, and cast down their napkins to the seats of their red plush chairs. Businessmen, their deals concluded, offered each other a toast. Crystal clinked on crystal; wine flowed, dark as Our Saviour's blood. Fludd opened his mouth to speak, began, and broke off. His throat ached with pity. 'I should like to tell you,' he said at last. 'For my own reasons, I cannot.'

'What kind of reasons?'

'You might say, professional ones.'

Because in the work of transformation, there are conditions of success. The art requires the whole man; and besides the alembics and retorts, the furnace and the charcoal, there must be knowledge and faith, gentle speech and good works. And then when all of these are brought together, there must be one further thing, guarantor of all the rest: there must be silence.

Fludd looked around the room, attracted the attention of the waiter, signalled that they were ready for their next course. The waiter brought other plates, and then a little spirit-burner, which he set up on their table. He whipped his white napkin around in an ostentatious way, and flipped it over his arm; he seemed to be looking around, out of the corner of his eye, to see whether his colleagues were observing him.

Then some meat came along, in a sauce, and Roisin O'Halloran watched the waiter put it over the spirit-burner to warm it up for them; then he poured something over it. A moment later he set fire to the whole lot. Her cheeks burned in embarrassment for him. It was something even Sister Anthony had never managed. On the stove, yes, often: not at the very table.

But Fludd didn't seem to mind. He looked at her steadily from behind the blaze. She supposed the meat would still be edible, and she would try to get through it: to please him.

At that moment when the blue flame leapt up between them, illuminating the starched white cloth and his dark face, tears sprang into her eyes. This is all very well, she thought, while it lasts, but it won't last, will it, because even

Hell comes to an end, and even Heaven. 'Champagne,' Fludd said to the waiter. 'Come on man, look lively, didn't I order champagne?'

When she woke next morning, and the bed was empty, she cried a little; in fright and panic, like a sleepy child in a strange room. It did not surprise her that she had slept so soundly that she had not heard him go; it had been a willed, furious sleep, the kind of sleep that perhaps felons have the night before they are hanged.

She got out of bed, stiffly, and naked, groped about on the dressing table. Sunlight crept around the edges of the heavy curtains. She looked about the room; she was casting around for something, but she hardly knew what.

But very soon, she found what she was looking for. Her eye fell on a paper. He had left her a letter, it seemed.

The eiderdown had fallen to the floor. Roisin O'Halloran pulled a blanket from the bed, and wrapped it around her shoulders. She did not want to draw back the curtains; she switched on the lamp.

Then she took up the paper. She unfolded it. His writing was strange, black, cramped, old-fashioned, like a secret script. The letter was brief.

The gold is yours. You will find it in the drawer.

Not a word, not a word of love. Perhaps, she thought, he does not love in the ordinary way. God loves us, after all; He manifests it in cancer, cholera, Siamese twins. Not all forms of love are comprehensible, and some forms of love destroy what they touch.

She sat down on the bed with the piece of paper, holding it in both hands, as if it were some State Proclamation. She twisted her bare foot on the carpet, right and left, left and right. It was a slip of the pen, she thought, when he put 'gold'.

Presently she got up, laying the note down on the pillow.

She pulled open the top drawer of the tallboy, where his things had been. Now the drawer was almost empty.

But he had left her the railwayman's kerchief, which he had torn from the fence pole as he crossed the allotments on his way to the station. 'I left them something of my own,' he had said. 'I did not wish to go from the parish having made no mark.'

She picked the kerchief up, shook it out. She held it to her face. It smelled of peat and of coal fires, of fog and hen-houses, of the whole year past. She folded it up and laid it on the tallboy's polished top.

Apart from the kerchief there was nothing but a drawstring bag of grubby calico; the sort of bag the children kept their marbles in, but a good deal larger. She picked it up and felt it; it was bulky and heavy. She pulled at its mouth and stretched it open. Inside, banknotes.

Jesus, she thought, has he done some robbery? Is it spirit-money, or would they take it in the shops? She took the first sheaf out onto her lap and held it as if she were weighing it. It looked real enough. It seemed that those little sixpences that he had put into his handkerchief had multiplied. There were notes of a denomination she had never seen before.

Roisin O'Halloran emptied the bag. She turned the bundles about in her hands, and riffled their edges. She did not know how much cash there might be. It would be a body's work to count it. She felt sure that it would be enough for anything that she might want to buy.

So. She sat for a while, thinking about it. She wanted him back, yes; she imagined the hours, days, months, years, when her heart was going to ache. But leaving that aside, did she not feel remarkably consoled? After all, she would not be going begging to a farmer now. She would not be knocking on some convent door. Nobody would have to take her in and give her charity; not while this lasted, and with her frugal habits she thought it would last a great while. By the time this money runs out, she thought, I shall be somewhere else, somebody else; life will have its second chance with me.

And why indeed should it ever run out, was her next thought. This was no ordinary coin, or common gold. This money is like love, she thought at once. Once you have some, once it has come into being, it can go on multiplying, each part dividing itself, doubling and doubling like the cells of an embryo.

She glanced down at her paper wedding ring. I could get a real one, she said to herself. Her spirits rose. She picked up a wad of notes and pressed it to her cheek. And they say it's the root of all evil. Well, Protestants say that. Catholics know better.

She replaced the money, bit by bit, each sheaf nestling against its fellow; then she drew up the string, and put the whole carefully into the bottom of her Gladstone bag. Then she took the letter from the pillow and folded it, and put that in too. It was quite clear, if anyone should challenge her; the gold is yours, it said.

She stood at the washbasin, and watched hot water gush from the taps; she took her flannel and wetted it and squeezed it, and washed herself all over with scented soap, and then let the water out, and refilled the basin, and washed herself again with water that was clear and almost cold. People live like this, she thought. Every morning they can get up and do this if they want.

She dressed herself. There was only the costume to put on. She had become used to it. After all, she thought, there are more important things to worry you than what other people think.

She made the bed; then she sat down on it, and cried for five minutes. She timed it by the clock; she felt it was as much as she should be allowed. Because she had known he would leave her; she did not imagine it could have been different.

When her five minutes were up she went to the washbasin for a last time, ran a corner of the flannel under the cold tap, and bathed her eyes. She straightened up and looked at herself in the mirror. She tied on her checked headscarf; public opinion might not matter, but she told herself that it would be a pity if she were taken up and sent to an asylum. Then she drew back the curtains. A great wave of sunlight poured into the room, and washed over the wardrobe and the tallboy and the newly made bed. She stepped back and looked at it in astonishment.

Then timidly, she quit the room, and crept down the corridor; past the large windows curtained with grease and soot, and then with greying net: with crimson velvet drapes restrained by gold ropes and tassels, like a cardinal's hat in a coat of arms. She descended the wide stone staircase, and approached the mahogany altar: behind which the personage stood, and gave her a civil greeting. She offered to settle the bill: to which the personage, much surprised, said that the doctor had already done that. Where was the doctor, he wanted to know? Already left, she said.

Oh, I see, then we'd better have you out of here right away, *Mrs* Fludd, the man said. She noticed that his manner had changed, and become markedly less civil; but she simply said, mildly, that she was leaving at once, did he not see that she had her bag? Oh you could have called a porter, *Madam*, the personage said, you wouldn't want to strain yourself: and when she had handed him the key, and was crossing the slippery expanse of the foyer, that waste of marble like a iced lake, she heard him say to some colleague of his, well, would you credit it, Tommy, I thought I could spot one a mile off, I've never seen such a bloody strange-looking tart in twenty years in the hotel trade.

It was one of those days, rare in the north of England, when a pale sun picks out every black twig of a winter tree; when a

ground-frost forms a gilded haze over the pavements, and
great buildings, the temples of commerce, shimmer as if their
walls were made of air and smoke. Then the city casts off its
grim arctic character, and its denizens their sourness and
thrift; the grace of affability dawns on their meagre features,
as if the pale sun had warmth in it, and power to kindle
hearts. Then office workers long to hear Mozart, and eat
Viennese pastries, and drink coffee scented with figs. Clean-
ing women hum behind their mops, and click their stout
heels like flamenco dancers. Canaletto pauses on Blackfriars
Bridge, to take a perspective; gondoliers ply their trade on
the Manchester Ship Canal.

Roisin O'Halloran hurried to the station. She passed under
the great advertisers' hoardings that wound their way up
London Road, and if anyone noticed her blue serge suit, and
her black plimsolls, they took them as part of the novelty of
the day. Her eyes stung and her cheeks burned; but it was an
exhilarating cold, and everything about her – the gilded
pavements, the faces of Mancunians, the coloured pictures
above her head – seemed to her to have been freshly created
– made overnight, manufactured by some new and ingenious
process that left them clean and hard-edged and resplendent,
faces immaculate, hoardings immaculate, pavements without
a stain. I could go anywhere, she thought. Back to Ireland.
On a boat. If I liked. Or not.

When she entered London Road Station, its clamorous
darkness full of smoke and steam, its railway noises breaking
like waves against the roof, she put her bag down carefully,
between her feet, and looked up at the destination boards.
Then she picked one out.

Father Angwin woke late; Miss Dempsey brought him tea in
bed, the first time in all their years together that she had ever
done such a thing. The Children of Mary would be scan-
dalized, she thought, if they knew I was in a priest's bedroom

while the priest was in his bed. Perhaps I would be drummed out, and disgraced for ever.

Anyway, it would prepare him to face what the day must bring: questions, circumventions, realizations. The time will come, she thought, when we will look back on what has occurred, and account it an Age of Miracles. She touched the spot where her wart used to be; these last two days, whenever she passed a looking-glass – and she had plans to hang many more – she would pause, and gaze at herself, and smile.

Meanwhile there were the police to be dealt with. At nine o'clock the Chief Constable came in person. He was a modern policeman, fresh-faced and cold-eyed, and he liked nothing better than to tear around the county in his big black car.

In paintings, there are various guises in which angels come to make their annunciation. Some have bird-bones and tiny feet, and wings that shimmer like a kingfisher's back. Others, with delicate, crimped gold hair, have the demure expression of music-mistresses. Some angels appear more masculine. Their feet, huge and simian, dig into the marble pavements. Their wings have the wet solidity of large marine animals.

There is a painting, a Virgin and Child, by Ambrogio Bergognone. The woman has a silvery pallor; her child is plump and well-doing, the kind of baby, ready to walk if it were not so idle, that makes your arms ache. She supports him with one hand; his feet are set upon a deep green cloth.

On either side of her is an open window, giving out on to a dusty street. Life goes on; in the distance is a bell-tower. Approaching, a figure carries a basket. Walking away from us are two other figures, absorbed in conversation, and following them closely is a small white dog with a plumed tail. The infant plays with a string of rosary beads: coral, perhaps.

An open book is propped before the woman. She is reading the First Psalm, with its message of utter reassurance: 'For the Lord knoweth the ways of the just; and the ways of the wicked shall perish.'

The Virgin's expression, at first sight, seems unfathomably

sad. It is only on closer observation that one notices the near-smirk on her dimpled mouth, and the expression of satisfaction in her long, dun-coloured eyes.

About the author

Read on

Ideas,
interviews
& features ...

A Kind of Alchemy

Sarah O'Reilly talks to Hilary Mantel

What made you a writer, and when did you realise that writing was where your future lay?
I realised quite late in life, as these things go. A lot of people know they're going to be writers when they're children, but I made a conscious decision to become one when I was 22, when, because of my poor health, I saw other career prospects slipping away from me. I knew I could write – you couldn't take the decision otherwise – but what I didn't know was whether I could write fiction. I didn't seem to be what people call a 'natural storyteller'. I had to learn that bit.

What was your first novel, and when was it written?
The first book I wrote was *A Place of Greater Safety*, though it wasn't published until 1992. I wrote two drafts of it in the 1970s in Botswana, and had completed it, or so I thought, by the end of 1979. I had spent five years writing it, then set myself a revision schedule of 15 pages a day. No matter how ill I was, I wouldn't let myself depart from that. I came home to England with the manuscript in the hope of selling it to somebody, but suddenly my health collapsed, totally. Which just shows the power of the imagination. The book was dragging me along, and then once I'd written the last full stop that was it – I was jelly.

**A Place of Greater Safety was initially
turned down by publishers. How did the
book eventually make it into print?**

My collapse was followed by a great period
of readjustment and change in my life. I put
my health back together, and went to Saudi
Arabia with my husband, where I wrote a
completely different kind of book [*Every
Day is Mother's Day*, followed by its sequel
Vacant Possession] and consigned *A Place of
Greater Safety* to the shelf, where it stayed.
I had successfully published four other
books and was writing another, *A Change
of Climate*, when my friend Clare Boylan
rang me about a feature she was writing for
the *Guardian* newspaper about writers'
unpublished first novels. She asked me if I
had one, and I had a very strong impulse to
lie. I knew that if I said yes it would have
consequences. The novel was my dark secret
– it had been a long time since I'd looked
at it, and I was afraid that it would be
unviable. Plus my career appeared to be
moving on in quite a satisfactory way, and
it was hard to see how this enormous
historical novel would fit into the logic of
what I had already published. Behind it all
was the fear that if I reread it and I felt it
didn't work as a novel, it would mean I'd
wasted some of the best years of my life, my
twenties, slaving over it.

But of course I had to realise that I'd not
been happy with that book sitting on the
shelf. I'd been contented with my career, but
not happy; pleased with the way things ▶

6 It's a very
powerful and
mysterious idea,
that one thing
can absolutely be
another, that the
world as you
perceive it is a
kind of mirage 9

A Kind of Alchemy *(continued)*

◄ had gone, but not satisfied. So I said yes to Clare and the article appeared, and predictable consequences followed. My agent and my publisher asked to see a copy of the manuscript, and the book was accepted for publication in the autumn of that year. This meant I had one summer to go through and make revisions, so after years of inactivity there was suddenly a huge rush to prepare it for the printers. I suspect that summer changed my orientation to my work because it was only by becoming a workaholic that I managed to get it done.

When I think of the book now, I realise that the proper thing for me to do was to put it out there, to let people know that, though I had published four contemporary novels, I was something else as well: an accumulator and sifter and sorter of facts, dates and research. It was time to show that there was a whole other side to my writing personality.

That writing personality has been expressed through many forms – short stories, historical novels, a memoir – and has ranged over a number of periods and places. Surveying your literary hinterland, can you detect a unifying, overarching theme in your work?
I think all of my books are really about a kind of alchemy, on a personal level. I was brought up a Catholic and that's a very hard thing to shake off. In an ideal world all writers would have a Catholic childhood, or belong to some other religion which does

the equivalent for you, because Catholicism tells you at a very early age that the world is not what you see; that in fact beyond appearances there is another reality, and it is a far more important reality. I was taught Catholic doctrine at an age when my imagination was still forming, and I think that the idea of transubstantiation – where you are told that one thing can change into another thing, all in a moment, whilst its appearance remains the same – is very powerful. It makes you fixate on the moment when the change takes place, and the nature of that change; the moment where the thing that still looks like a piece of bread is actually the body of God. It's a very powerful and mysterious idea, that one thing can absolutely be another, that the world as you perceive it is a kind of mirage. And if you put ideas like that into a child's head they do their work.

In *A Place of Greater Safety*, which is set in the midst of a political revolution, I ask, 'What is the moment at which there's no going back?' In terms of the three main characters I ask, 'Is there a moment when life changes decisively, where there is absolutely no return to the person you were before, or the conditions as they were?' In the case of one of my characters, Camille Desmoulins, I think the answer is yes, there is a moment of transubstantiation. He became famous in an instant, and after that he walks and talks and looks like Camille but he is *not* Camille, he is someone different. Then the question carries over into how an individual can, by the force of ▶

6 *Fludd* was written with a child's-eye view, so that you have very miraculous things appearing to happen very ordinarily, and very ordinary things appearing miraculous 9

5

A Kind of Alchemy *(continued)*

◄ their will, make themselves over into something or someone other, and I am fascinated by people who have this tremendous force of will. Carmel McBain in *An Experiment in Love* has it, as does Robespierre in *A Place of Greater Safety*, and Thomas Cromwell in *Wolf Hall*. Each of these characters forces personal revolutions, which have to be made, and remade, every day. In *Fludd*, I make the theme overt with my use of alchemy as the novel's supporting metaphor, though I think that it's really present in all my books.

You first published *Fludd* in 1989, three years before *A Place of Greater Safety* made it into print. Can you talk a little about how the story of the havoc wreaked on the sleepy village of Fetherhoughton by the mysterious arrival of the curate – devil? – Fludd came to you?
The first thing to say is that my novels often appear in big overlapping patterns, so that I might be working on one in my head and another on the page. *Fludd* came out of a conversation with my mother about Hadfield, the village where I grew up, which is reimagined as Fetherhoughton in the novel, and its adjacent hamlet Padfield, which is reimagined as Netherhoughton. One thing we discussed was how, when I was around four years old, the bishop decreed that all the statues which filled the church, familiar presences to the parishioners, were to be removed.

The bishop's decree made him hugely unpopular, and I remember the sense of scandal and upset expressed by adults talking above my head. My mother proposed to adopt one of the statues, and take it into our home. Another voice asked, 'Well, what are they going to do with them?' The answer, 'They're going to bury them', sent a shudder through me. So there was that matter. Then my mother said to me, during this reminiscence, 'Another funny thing was that there was a young priest who came and everyone really liked him, and then suddenly he vanished, and we supposed there was a girl involved.' After I left my mother, I got on the train to London and these stories began to work on me, to the point where by the end of the journey I had written the first and last sentence of the book in my mind, with the rest to be reimagined. Then I just had to put the novel in the queue.

The idea of the mystery that lies beyond the visible world is something that runs through your fiction. In *Fludd* the mystery collects around a stranger to the parish, but it's also explored at length in *Beyond Black*. Absolutely, yes. *Fludd* was written with a child's-eye view, so that you have very miraculous things appearing to happen very ordinarily, and very ordinary things appearing miraculous. It's to do with a child's sense of what magic is, and when I wrote it I wanted to recapture that mindset, though of course I didn't really have to try, I just fell straight back into the world of Hadfield, and the way it seemed to me from a knee-high point of view. ▶

6 I feel as if I'm conscious all the time of different realities that are forming and reforming and humming about one's head, and this restless and quite frightening idea creeps into *Fludd* 9

A Kind of Alchemy *(continued)*

◀ The mystery that lies behind the visible world is certainly the central preoccupation in *Beyond Black*, which is where I take on the subject explicitly – is the world as we see it, or are there competing and overlapping realities? I am a fan of the latter concept, but I have to phrase this carefully so as not to sound mad. I feel as if I'm conscious all the time of different realities that are forming and reforming and humming about one's head, and this restless and quite frightening idea creeps into *Fludd* but absolutely suffuses *Beyond Black*.

In virtually all my books there's a slight edge of the supernatural, and a preoccupation with what is hidden, what may be in the locked room. The locked room may be part of the psyche; it may be the part of the imagination that one doesn't dare enter.

The question of what is hidden or buried in our past is a central theme in *A Change of Climate*, published in 1994. Can you talk a little about how the book came about? And were there two stories, as in the case of *Fludd*, that joined together in your mind to create the novel?

In *A Change of Climate* there's the central secret, the enormous, destructive secret that the Eldreds bury. They've not been able to bury their child but they've buried their experience, which they can do because it is something that happened in Africa, a place which, to their friends in England, is in any case in the realms of the inexplicable. Africa becomes a metaphor for what we do not explore; in the novel it's no longer a solid place that one can travel to, but somewhere consigned to the subconscious.

The idea for the book came to me in two parts. When I went to Botswana in 1977 the first thing I did was sit and read the law reports and it was there that I first came across medicine murders and the theft of children. I squirrelled the information away, not knowing how I would use it, until I heard one day of an apparently happily married couple who had suddenly split up, after doing all the hard work of bringing up a family. Why? I remember asking my friends this question when the two parts of the story suddenly came together in my mind.

Have you ever been surprised by anything you've written?

In a way I feel, more than with any other book, that I have absolutely no responsibility for what I put on the page in *The Giant, O'Brien*. When I first came across a reference to the story of the real eighteenth-century giant, Charles O'Brien, I imagined that I would write a big, realistic historical novel about John Hunter, the great surgeon, collector and experimentalist who acquired his skeleton for research. We know a great deal about John, and I envisaged that the story of the giant would be the climax of the book. Yet when I sat down to write it something completely different happened: I heard the voices of the men in the cave.

I'd hit mid life, and suddenly I remembered – this will sound extraordinary – that I was Irish! My grandmother came ▶

6 Social convention allows the medium and the writer to talk to the dead, and our occupations are seen as respectable forms of economic activity, by which I mean ones on which we must pay income tax 9

A Kind of Alchemy *(continued)*

◀ from a very large Irish Catholic family
but she was at the young end of it, so by
the time I was ten almost all my Irish
relatives on this side of the Irish Sea were
dead. The result was that as I grew up I
completely lost my sense of being Irish,
until I began to think about this book. It
was as if I woke up one day, and was
suddenly hit with the knowledge that below
the language I was speaking there was
another language, a language that had been
lost. Somehow the giant's story became part
of this awakening, and the feeling grew in
me that in order to find myself I had to go
back and capture that voice, that Irishness.
So the novel became about the giant utterly,
and the giant's people, and the giant's
transition from speaking Irish to speaking
English, exploring what is lost, and what is
gained in the process. It was as if something
came into the room, opened its mouth, and
sang. I just wrote the song out and it was
over.

**Beyond Black tells the story of Alison, a
medium who is plagued by the voices of
the dead. Given your description of the way
in which your characters communicate
with you, I wonder whether you feel an
affinity of sorts with Alison's predicament?**
Very much so, yes. Only the medium and
the writer are licensed to sit in a room by
themselves with a whole crowd of imaginary
people, listening and responding to them.
Social convention allows the medium and
the writer to talk to the dead, and our
occupations are seen as respectable forms of

economic activity, by which I mean ones on which we must pay income tax. Of course, I think also that there's the element of public performance in both professions, this need to go out and ply your strange trade in public. Through Alison I was making overt what my experience of writing novels has been, and my experience of living in the competing realities of the solid flesh-and-blood world and the layers of voices, and other realities, that demand your attention. Of course for me the object is to be serene and not let people see that there's mayhem going on inside. *Beyond Black* is about the terror of living below consciousness, of going down every day and every night into the realm where the demons are and where the bodies are buried. It's what the writer does all the time. ■

Author photograph © John Haynes

LIFE
at a Glance

BORN
Derbyshire, 1952

EDUCATED
Village school, convent grammar, LSE and Sheffield University

FAMILY
Married, no children

CAREER
Patchy: social worker, shop assistant, barmaid, teacher, film critic, novelist

A Writing Life

When do you write?
Whenever an idea strikes.

Where do you write?
Wherever I am. Usually on public transport.

Why do you write?
Good question. Habit / need to earn money / curiosity about what I will say next / hope of doing something good.

Pen or computer?
Pen first, as I write all ideas in notebooks initially. But the screen seems as natural as paper.

Silence or music?
Sometimes I put on music, but I screen it out; I only hear it if my writing is not flowing.

How do you start?
With spirit and dash, but with an error: I usually rewrite the beginning.

And finish?
Softly. I have to go back after a few days and work it up.

Do you have any writing rituals?
None.

Who is your favourite living writer?
Oliver Sacks.

If you weren't a writer, what would you do?
I'd be a spy.

Have You Read?

Other books by Hilary Mantel

A Place of Greater Safety
Amid the rising tides of the French
Revolution, three men taste the addictive
delights of power. Two are ambitious young
lawyers, the third a genius of rhetoric,
charming and handsome, erratic and
untrustworthy. Together Danton, Robespierre
and Desmoulins find themselves in the
centre of a gathering storm, unleashing the
darker side of the Revolution's ideals and
experiencing the horrors that follow.

'Superbly readable . . . An assured and
strange masterpiece' *Sunday Telegraph*

A Change of Climate
The Eldreds live in the Red House in
Norfolk, raising their four children and
devoting their lives to charity. But a crisis is
growing in the family. Memories of their time
as missionaries in southern Africa, and of the
tragedy that has shaped their lives, refuse to
be put to rest, threatening to destroy the
fragile peace they have built for themselves
and their children. As the past seeps into the
present, the Eldreds must face the most
punishing questions. Is there anything one
can never forgive? Is tragedy deserved? Can
you ever escape your own past?

'Mantel has created that rare thing, a page-
turner with a profound moral dimension'
                              Daily Telegraph ▶

Have You Read? *(continued)*

◄ *An Experiment in Love*
WINNER OF THE HAWTHORNDEN PRIZE
It is London, 1970, and Carmel McBain, in
her first term at university, has cut free
of her childhood roots in the North.
Among the gossiping, flirtatious girls of
Tonbridge Hall, Carmel begins her
experiments in love and life. But the year
turns. The miniskirt falls out of fashion
and an era of concealment begins. Carmel's
world darkens. Tragedy waits in the wings.

'The most powerful of all her novels, a
near-faultless masterpiece of pathos,
observation and feeling' *Sunday Telegraph*

....

The Giant, O'Brien
John Hunter, celebrated surgeon and
anatomist, buys dead bodies from the
gallows and babies' corpses by the inch.
The surprising Irish Giant – Charles
O'Brien – may be the sensation of the
season, but where is a man to hide his
bones when he is still alive?

'Mantel writes about curiosity,
companionship, art, love, death and
eternity. She writes with wit, compassion
and great elegance. Her books never fail to
surprise, nor to delight: in this one she is at
her very best – so far'
Independent on Sunday

....

Giving Up the Ghost
In this extraordinary memoir, Hilary Mantel
reclaims the ghosts that have come to haunt

her. From childhood daydreams to family secrets, her father's mysterious disappearance and an adulthood blighted by medical neglect, Mantel uncovers the losses that wrenched her from the patterns of the past and drove her to forge her own remarkable path.

'A masterpiece'   *Guardian*

Beyond Black

Alison Hart, a medium by trade, tours the dormitory towns of London's orbital road with her flint-hearted sidekick Colette, passing on messages from dead ancestors. But behind her plump, smiling persona is a desperate woman: the next life holds terrors that she must conceal from her clients, and her own waking hours are plagued by the spirits of men from her past. They infiltrate her house, her body and her soul, and the more she tries to be rid of them, the stronger and nastier they become . . .

'A brilliant, extraordinary book'
HELEN DUNMORE

Wolf Hall

WINNER OF THE 2009 MAN BOOKER PRIZE
'Lock Cromwell in a deep dungeon in the morning,' says Thomas More, 'and when you come back that night he'll be sitting on a plush cushion eating larks' tongues, and all the gaolers will owe him money.' It is the 1520s. Henry VIII is on the throne, but has no heir. Cardinal Wolsey, his chief adviser, ▶

Have You Read? *(continued)*

◄ is charged with securing the divorce the Pope refuses to grant. Into this atmosphere of distrust comes Thomas Cromwell, first as Wolsey's clerk, and later his successor. Cromwell is a wholly original man: the son of a brutal blacksmith, he is a political genius, a briber, a charmer, a bully, a man with a delicate and deadly expertise in manipulating people and events. Ruthless in pursuit of his own interests, he is equally ambitious in wider politics. His reforming agenda is carried out in the grip of a self-interested parliament and a king who fluctuates between romantic passions and murderous rages. With a vast array of characters, and richly overflowing with incident, *Wolf Hall* peels back history to show us Tudor England as a half-made society, moulding itself with great passion and suffering and courage.

'Majestically conjures up an England in the throes of epic change . . . a Great British Novel'   *Observer*

'A stunning book. It breaks free of what the novel has become nowadays. I can't think of anything since *Middlemarch* which so convincingly builds a world'

DIANA ATHILL ■